I'LL BE HOME SOON

OTHER BOOKS FOR YOUNG READERS
BY LUANNE ARMSTRONG

Pete's Gold (Ronsdale Press, 2008)

Into the Sun (Hodgepog Books, 2002)

Jeannie and the Gentle Giants (Ronsdale Press, 2001)

Maggie and Shine (Hodgepog Books, 1999)

Arly and Spike (Hodgepog Books, 1997)

Annie (Polestar Press, 1995)

I'll Be Home Soon

LUANNE ARMSTRONG

RONSDALE PRESS

I'LL BE HOME SOON
Copyright © 2012 Luanne Armstrong

RONSDALE PRESS
3350 West 21st Avenue, Vancouver, B.C., Canada V6S 1G7
www.ronsdalepress.com

Typesetting: Julie Cochrane, in Minion 12 pt on 16
Cover Art & Design: Nancy de Brouwer, Massive Graphic Design
Paper: Ancient Forest Friendly "Silva" (FSC)—100% post-consumer waste, totally chlorine-free and acid-free

Ronsdale Press wishes to thank the following for their support of its publishing program: the Canada Council for the Arts, the Government of Canada through the Canada Book Fund, the British Columbia Arts Council and the Province of British Columbia through the British Columbia Book Publishing Tax Credit program.

Library and Archives Canada Cataloguing in Publication

Armstrong, Luanne, 1949–
    I'll be home soon / Luanne Armstrong.

Issued also in electronic format.
ISBN 978-1-55380-180-1

    I. Title.

PS8551.R7638I45 2012   jC813'.54   C2012-902657-3

At Ronsdale Press we are committed to protecting the environment. To this end we are working with Canopy (formerly Markets Initiative) and printers to phase out our use of paper produced from ancient forests. This book is one step towards that goal.

Printed in Canada by Marquis Printing, Quebec

This book is dedicated to my mother,
Dorothy Anne Klingensmith Armstrong

ACKNOWLEDGEMENTS

Thanks to my writing group: Tanna Patterson,
Kelly Ryckman, Linda Breault, Ilana Cameron, Deryn
Collier and Kuya Minogue for ideas and suggestions.
Thanks to Neil Ripski for tips on kung fu. Thanks to
Eli Leary for information on street youth. Warmest
gratitude to the kind people of Eastend, Saskatchewan,
for a month's writing retreat at Wallace Stegner House
where this book began. Thanks to Dorothy Woodend
for support and editing suggestions.

Chapter One

REGAN CHECKED THE street behind her to make sure no one was looking at her. She ran into the alley, stopped at the fallen gate, picked her way through a backyard littered with bags of trash, twisted pieces of bicycles, rusty grocery carts, and broken glass. Blackberry vines and white-flowered morning glory were slowly eating it all up.

She climbed through a broken window into the abandoned house, picked her way past the lumps of human waste on the old wooden floor, up a broken staircase and out another window. Then she squatted on the roof of the porch, in the shadows, just under the overhang of the roof to watch the street.

She was watching for her mother. Watching relieved the ache for a bit. Someday very soon, her mother would walk down this street and Regan would see her. The front door to their apartment building was across the street. Regan hated their stuffy small apartment, with its smell of mouldy carpets. It didn't feel like home at all without her mother there. It was easier to sit here, where she could see everyone but no one could see her.

She knew just how it would be. She would see her mother coming; she would come down off the roof and run across the street. Her mother would throw her arms around Regan. "Baby," she would say, laughing, "I missed you too much."

And then they would go for fish and chips or fried chicken and her mother would explain everything and the world would be right-side-up again.

Three weeks ago her mother said, "Wait for me, I've got a chance to make some real money. I'll be home soon, back in two, three days. There's food for that long. Don't skip school." She had dressed in her best clothes, with her red high-heeled shoes. She had pinned up her long red hair and put on some silver earrings. And left, in a cloud of perfume and scent from her hairspray. And then she hadn't come back.

Regan had waited and gone to school and watched the street until she ran out of money for food. Then she began scrounging for food. She got up and dressed and went to school every day and came home and tried not to panic. She pretended everything was fine. Her mother had left before.

And she had always come back with a story and a purse full of money.

So this afternoon, yet again, Regan watched the street. She didn't have anything else to do. It was a grey Sunday and she sat far enough under the overhang of the roof to stay dry if it rained. Two grey squirrels fought in the huge maple tree beside the house; they ran up and down, over the branches, leaping from branch to branch.

She had been here many times before, but today when she had come in the alley, the trees had orange fencing around them. She knew what this meant. Very soon, bulldozers would push the house over. Enormous trucks would back up; everything, splintered and broken would be dumped, crashed and smashed into the back of those trucks, and then a new building would rise on this spot and no one would remember this house at all.

Except her. Once, Regan thought, the house must have been beautiful. Once it had housed a family. She could tell by what was left of it, by the sheen of the wood floors under the dung and rat turds, by the carved ornate banisters on the broken staircase, and by the air of dignity that still clung to the house despite its age and disrepair. She wished she could write an essay for English class about it. She would like to imagine a story about the house and about the life in it, a life with a family that had a mother and a father and a lot of food, food that was rich and warm and cooked in a house that smelled of love. Even a dog. A dog that had a lot of food as well. She had wanted to try sleeping in the house but she knew it wasn't safe, couldn't be made safe, and so, she didn't.

Down on the street, cars and people continued to pass in a steady stream. Men wheeled jangling, clinking shopping carts full of cans and bottles to the depot on the next block. Most of the men she had seen before. Old Annie went by with her own cart heaped with blankets and garbage bags stuffed with her treasures. She was on her way to the church for dinner, and this reminded Regan of her own hunger. Hunger she lived with. Some days she could push it away, keep moving but today wasn't one of those days. She was hungry enough—almost—to stand in line at the church with Annie, to accept a bowl of soup and a bun and a little packet of crackers. If she stood with Annie, Annie would talk to her, pretend they were together and no one would question her age. They would give her food.

But then Annie would start muttering to herself and people would look at Regan, and she wouldn't be able to eat her soup and dry bun fast enough and get out of there. No, she couldn't face it today. She could go up the hill to the grocery store that left food out at night, the store that didn't lock its dumpsters. She'd have to wait until dark, but then she could bring food back to the apartment and eat it all by herself. That's what she would do.

Or she could just wait here. Go on waiting for her mother. When her mother came, Regan would tell her about waiting. And her mother would be pleased that Regan had been so enterprising and independent and hadn't asked for a handout or help from anyone. Her mother believed in independence. Eventually Regan even slept a little, crouched on the roof, her arms wrapped around her knees. She had stayed awake, reading, late into last night, in order to keep the silence of the dark apartment at bay.

She woke with a start. It was really raining now and getting dark. It would take her an hour to walk up the hill to the dumpster with food and then an hour back and she would be soaked when she got home. But she was hungry enough that it would be worthwhile. She started to stand up, and then stopped. Two people were yelling out in the alley. They were behind a tree and she couldn't see them, but she could tell it was a man and a woman. She didn't want to get caught in anyone else's argument; she'd seen enough of those. There was always something going on in the street and she knew enough to stay far away from that kind of violence.

Eventually the man grabbed the woman by the arm and pulled her, still screaming, down the alley and out to the street. In a few minutes, a police cruiser went by. When everything was quiet, Regan climbed off the roof, went out through the yard and trudged up the street on her way to get some food.

The next morning, she woke early in the dark cold apartment. She could hear that it was still raining. She curled under the covers, still cold. It had taken hours for her to get warm after she had made it home and wolfed down some bread and cheese and yogurt. Should she go to school? Should she even bother? The problem was, the more school she missed, the harder it got to relate to whatever the teacher was droning on about. The other kids had started making fun of her. She needed a lot of things like better shoes and clean clothes. She had no coins for the laundromat. Mostly, she needed her mother to come back.

She sighed and sat up. She stood for a long time under the hot shower, got dressed as fast as she could, pulling on layer after layer of her least dirty clothes. She gulped down some more bread and cheese and headed for school. But outside she stopped and stood, staring at the pavement.

What she wanted was for her mother to come back and deal with everything for her. And what she also needed, right now, was a way to figure out what to do, where to look for her. She'd been thinking about this for days but she needed an idea of where to start. She needed someone to hash things over with, someone who knew the streets, who would make sense and tell her what to do and where to look. Was there such a person?

But she also knew she couldn't stand the thought of going to school in her damp clothes, sitting all day and coming home alone to a dark cold apartment. She had to do something. Sitting on a roof waiting for her mother wasn't working.

"Hey Reggie."

Oh no, she thought. Not this person.

"Hi Sarah," she said, and forced a smile. Of all the people

to run into, it was the street youth worker, the last person she wanted to see. Because if Sarah knew Regan's mother was gone, she'd call a social worker. And that would mean trouble.

"How's it going? Everything okay?"

Sarah was tall with curly black hair. She had a round strong brown face and right now she was beaming kindness and care at Regan.

"Yeah, fine."

"How's your mom?"

"Good."

Sarah studied Regan with a practised eye. "You on your way to school? How are you liking grade eight? Want me to walk you a ways? Or I could buy you breakfast."

Breakfast. What she wouldn't give for a hot breakfast. And she had kung fu tonight for which she would need all her strength . . . and they hadn't paid Sifu for the last two months either.

"Naw, that's okay, I'm kind of in a hurry."

"Right, that's why you were standing here studying the sidewalk so hard."

Regan sighed. "I gotta go, Sarah, okay?"

"Aw c'mon, big, hot breakfast. You can be late for school for once, hey?"

Regan hesitated. The bread and cheese she had eaten at the apartment hadn't filled the hole in her belly. She could lie enough to Sarah to get through breakfast, although normally she hated lying. She nodded.

Sarah led the way to a grubby diner with steamed-up

windows. Once inside, she ordered coffee while Regan ordered the largest breakfast special they had. They sat in uncomfortable silence until the food came, and then Regan stuffed her mouth as fast as she could. Even when she was done, she was still hungry.

"Want some more?" Sarah waved at the waitress. "Two pieces of apple pie with ice cream, please."

Regan kept her head down. The warmth and the food were making her weak. She could feel the tears just behind her eyes.

"Regan, I gotta ask. You keep an eye out around here, yeah?"

Regan nodded.

"You know there's some serious stuff going down. I hear all kinds of weird rumours . . . people disappearing, gangs, crap like that. Worse than usual, although this is always a harsh place for women and kids. But I guess you know that already, huh?"

Regan stared at her. She knew Sarah wouldn't miss the flash of fear on her face and she didn't. She shook her head.

"You know them Dunster kids over on Main. They go to school with you, right?"

Regan nodded.

"Their mom has disappeared. I'm on my way over there now to pick them up, take them somewhere safe. Listen, you hear anything weird or unusual, or you have any trouble with anything, you let me know, huh."

Regan nodded. She stared out the window. In spite of herself, one tear rolled out of her eye and slid down her cheek.

"Okay, whoa, what do you know? What aren't you telling me? Is it your mom? Is everything okay? What's up, kiddo?"

"I gotta go," Regan said. She gritted her teeth and slid out of the booth. "I'm late for school."

"Hey, your aura is looking pretty dull," Sarah called after her. "Want me to read the runes for you?"

Regan just shook her head, turned and left. If Sarah liked to pretend she had psychic powers, that was up to her. Regan had more important things to attend to.

Sarah didn't say anything more. Regan paused at the door and looked back. Sarah was still watching her. Regan knew Sarah wouldn't give up. She'd come by the apartment later, maybe talk to the landlord. She'd figure out that Regan's mom had gone, and the next thing, Regan would be shut up in some crappy group home. No way, she thought. If she needed to disappear, that's what she would do. But then how would her mom find her when she did come home? Oh no, she thought. Mom, come home. Save me.

Chapter Two

IT TOOK HER MOST of the morning to find Mike. When she did find him, he was busking on the street, juggling—not very well—clowning, talking to the few people who showed any interest. He stopped when he saw her.

"Why, it's the princess," he said. His silver earrings flashed in the light; he had a new one in the top of his ear, she saw, plus another one through his eyebrow. He was wearing a torn black t-shirt, too-tight blue jeans, and sandals. His black curly hair stuck out in wiry corkscrews all around his tanned brown face. He looked grown up but Regan knew he was only sixteen. He had told her once, and then told her to keep it quiet.

"Just a minute," he said. "Almost done."

He threw a few more balls into the air, passed a hat, gained a few quarters and loonies, stuck the hat on his head and threw the juggling balls and other paraphernalia into a worn red gym bag covered with Coke logos.

"Let's go," he said. "You got your serious face on. I can tell something's up."

"Go where?" she asked, falling into step beside him.

"I dunno, it's a nice day, let's walk and talk, figure something out. Want anything? Need to escape reality for once?"

"No," she said. "You know I don't do that crap."

"Yeah, yeah, you and your see-saw, or whatever he is. Stay pure, stay clean, run away."

"Sifu," she said. "He's smart. And yeah, he's clean and no, he doesn't run away."

"I thought he told you not to fight."

"He told us not to pick fights. That's different."

"Yeah, yeah." He had already lost interest. He was like that, always flickering in and out. It was like being friends with a flame. When he turned his interest on something, it was with total intensity, but when he lost interest, he just moved on. So far, she had held his interest mostly by not seeing him very often.

"So, what's up?"

Regan wondered what to tell him. He had a big mouth but he knew a lot. He got around, Mike did. He knew the streets and most of the people living on them.

"It's my mom," she said, carefully controlling her voice. "Uh, she's not well, she went out a while back with some guy named Clayton, I think, and she's not back yet. I need to figure out how to look for her."

He didn't say anything, just kept walking, and then he said, "Go to the cops."

"What?"

"Go to the cops."

"Why?"

"Why?" He stopped and turned to face her. "Some things you can't deal with on your own, no matter what old see-saw says, some things you gotta have help with. This is your mother, for frick's sake. Go to the cops."

"But they'll stick me in a group home."

"Yeah, group homes are crap, but they'll feed you. You're too skinny now. You look like a strong wind would pick you up and dump you out in that disgusting filthy harbour."

"You hated group homes. You said you would never go back to one, no matter what."

"Yeah, well, that was me. Whatever. It's your life, princess. Do what you want."

He turned away and started walking again. She hesitated, wondering whether to follow.

"C'mon," he said impatiently.

"Where are we going?"

"A place I know, some people doing stuff." He turned. "Not drugs, just a place, some food, people, maybe it'll even be warm."

They walked down the hills and across the bridge. The sun came out and it was warm. Around them the city bustled and clanked and roared and spun and sparkled. Buses full of people went by, plus a solid wall of cars. Out on the ocean, freighters rested in the bay, gulls wheeled and screamed.

At the end of the bridge, Mike jumped off the sidewalk and led the way down the bank and onto a thin trail that wove through thick brush. They ducked under a bent and torn steel fence and scrambled down another bank, through tangled blackberry bushes, through some more brush, and into a small clearing that was almost directly under the bridge. A fire was burning; there were several brightly coloured tents. About ten people, mostly men, were sitting around the fire, some on chairs, some on logs. There was only one woman, huge, with a long red skirt and several brightly coloured shawls wrapped around her shoulders. Her long black hair was braided with beaded ribbons.

"Hey Mike," a man grunted. "Pull up a log."

Mike and Regan sat awkwardly on logs beside the fire. A pot was balanced on two logs just beside the fire. One of the men leaned forward, lifted the lid, and stirred the contents.

"Soup's on," he announced. He lifted the pot with gloves, put it on a plank laid over two shopping carts, ladled out bowls for everyone, including Regan and Mike, put out a bowl of crackers, and sliced cheese off an enormous orange loaf. Regan figured he probably got his food from the same place she did. The cheese had mould on it, and the crackers were stale, but it was food.

The soup had lentils and vegetables. It was hot and filling. She wasn't hungry after her breakfast with Sarah but she ate it all anyway. Afterwards, someone passed around a joint and someone else had cigarettes but she ignored them and just watched the light on the water below the camp and worried about her mother. Mike was no longer sitting by the fire.

Oh no, she suddenly thought, what if her mother had come home while she was sitting here and was looking for her.

She looked around. Mike was standing with another man beside one of the brightly coloured tents. They were talking urgently with their heads close together. Something changed hands between them.

She went and stood beside him. He glanced at her, annoyed at being interrupted.

"Mike," she whispered. "I gotta go home, maybe my mom is back by now."

"Okay, I'll come with you," he said. "I'll see you later," he said to the man who only nodded.

They said their goodbyes and Regan noted the whole set-up for later. If she ever needed a place to hide, if . . . but no, she didn't finish that thought. But this could be it. She didn't know these people but it was a possibility to keep pocketed away in the back of her head, just in case.

They went back along the brush-choked path, up the bank to the bridge. At the top, Regan turned left to go back across the bridge but Mike grabbed her hand.

"No, c'mon," he said. "I got another place to go, then you

can go home. Come with me, Princess, it might be fun. We'll go party, forget about everything."

"I need to go home," she said. "I have kung fu class tonight. Loan me bus fare, please, Mike."

When she made it home, the apartment was as cold and dark and lonely as ever. She crawled into a chair, pulled a quilt around her shoulders, rocked back and forth. Mike's voice rang in her head: go to the cops, go to the cops. But her mom wouldn't want her to go to the cops. She could talk to Sarah. Or even Sifu. Someone.

"Help," she whispered into the musty silent air. "Help, help, help, help."

But it was time for class. She got her robe and her sash and stuffed them in her pack. They needed washing but there wasn't much she could do about that. She went down the street to the studio. She smiled and nodded at the other kids, then went out onto the gym floor to do her kicks, punches, and other warm-ups. Regan loved this class. It was the one time she felt sure of herself, in control, powerful.

After class, Sifu called her over. She had been dreading this moment. Sifu was short, dark and intense. His head was shaved. He walked with such assurance and balance that Regan was sure nothing ever bothered him. If a bus hit him on the road, the bus would shatter and Sifu would keep walking.

"Regan, sorry to ask, could your mom call me?"

"Sorry," she mumbled. Her face flamed. "We're a little short this month. She'll pay you as soon as she can."

"Hmmm," he said. "Okay, if money short, no worries, scholarship for a bit. Catch up later. Big competition coming. Next month. Extra training okay? Can you ask her?"

"Sure," she said. "That would be great."

"Need a note."

"Not a problem."

"Okay, next week, extra half hour after class, okay?"

"Right, thanks, Sifu." She bowed formally and he bowed back and she ran out of the room, her heart singing. Then she stopped, turned back. She would ask him for help, she would.

But he was already leaving, out the other door, pushing down the handlebar and disappearing into the night.

Chapter Three

"SCHOOL," ONE PART of her mind argued. "Go to school."

She liked school. She did well at it. She didn't like the other kids much and they didn't like her but she didn't care. Mostly she liked books and reading and writing. Her English teacher always commented on the quality of her writing. Most of all, she loved the library and its stacks of books and rows of available computers.

Some days she even liked math. And this morning she had been missing having school in her life, especially her English class, and a chance to work on a new story on the computers at school. She also wanted to go to the library for a new supply of books. School was something regular and ordinary and bright in her life. Okay, she was going to go. But wow, what would she give for some clean underwear, a new shirt, even new socks.

If her mom were here, Regan would say she needed new clothes, and they'd go shopping at Value Village. They'd catch the bus and then they'd wander together around the store, trying on silly things and giggling and then they would have lunch and then they'd go home and all would be well.

Regan could almost see her mom, standing across the street, on the corner, waving and laughing, smoking a cigarette, and tossing her hair. Her mom was tall and thin with dyed red hair—she liked to laugh. "You have to laugh," she'd tell Regan. "Otherwise, life will kick your head in." Sometimes she laughed a bit too much, and then Regan would go quiet until her mom calmed down.

And her mom had had quite a few kicks. Regan didn't know all the stories, just some of them. How her dad had been killed in a logging accident in a small town when Regan was two. They'd been so happy, her mom said. Living in a small rented house, her dad making money, and the two of them saving up for a house of their own.

Regan didn't remember much of her younger life. After her dad was killed, they went to live with his mother and then Regan's mother disappeared for a while. Regan could remember that, could remember her grandmother sitting beside the kitchen table, staring out the window, while Regan played quietly in the corner with a pile of stuffed animals. She liked to tell the stuffed animals stories and have them tell her stories. She remembered that too.

And then things got confused. Her mom came back and then she and Regan's grandmother had a fight, and they moved and moved again. Men came and went, forgettable men with interchangeable faces. Her mom went from job to job. Finally, they ended up here, following yet another man who disappeared. Regan went from one school to another, and at each school there was the same trouble to fit in, find a friend or two, keep up with schoolwork. The library was always the safest place to be.

And yet her mom was more hopeful during this move, less despairing. Although their apartment was small and dark, her mom had promised that soon they would move to a nicer place, as soon as they got settled and as soon as she got a better job.

"Things are looking up, Regan. Things will get better." Her mom even signed up for some bookkeeping and accounting courses at a local college; she went out less and she and Regan spent more time together.

"My little queenie," her mom called her. "You know that's why I named you Regan. Because it means queen." And when she was home and Regan was getting ready for school, her mom would comb Regan's long, blond-brown hair and do it up in braids and put jewelled clips on the sides and Regan would feel, briefly, like a young queen.

Her mom had gone away before. "You don't mind, Regan," she'd always say. "It's just for a few days." She'd leave food in the fridge and a few bills clipped to the fridge. And then Joe or Jim or George would drive up, and her mom, smelling of perfume and hairspray, would wave and be gone. For a few days.

Not three weeks.

Regan blinked. It wasn't her mom on the street corner, but a gaggle of prostitutes, their heads together, cigarettes in hand, talking furiously. She went past them, down the street to the school, made it to her locker, made it through the day, all the while with a hollow empty fear echoing inside her like a drum, so that she could scarcely hear what the teacher or the kids were saying to her. When they first moved to the city, she hadn't understood why these women were always standing around on the street; the girls at her school had laughed at her ignorance. Now, whenever she saw them, she tried not to stare, tried not to think about them at all.

Her last class of the day was English, her favourite class, and her favourite teacher. Mary Harris, young, pretty, funny. She had told Regan that she thought Regan was a good writer, that she liked her stories, that she should think about being a writer when she grew up.

But today Regan couldn't pay attention. They were talking about some poem. She liked poetry but this one didn't make any sense. Regan kept thinking furiously that she had to do something, but her thoughts went around and around, repeating themselves over and over. Do something. But what? Do something.

The class finally ended and Regan gathered her books into her backpack, the panic rising in her throat like nausea, and made for the door.

"Regan," Mrs. Harris said. "Regan, come here please."

She almost didn't stop, so intent was she on running home to see if her mother was there, and if she wasn't, on running out again, somewhere, anywhere, to get help. She was desperate enough even to track down Sarah and ask her what to do.

"Regan, honey, are you okay? You're white as a sheet. Sit down."

Regan stopped, turned, came back slowly, and flopped into the chair beside the teacher's desk. She wanted to cry but she had long ago trained herself never to cry in front of strangers. "Never show weakness," her mom had said. "Or people will take advantage of you." Regan didn't know what her mom really meant, but she had an instinctive mistrust of strangers.

Mrs. Harris wasn't really a stranger though.

Regan swallowed the big lump in her throat.

"It's my mom," she said. "She hasn't been home in a while and I'm scared."

Mrs. Harris nodded slowly. "I see. How long is a while?"

"Maybe . . . a couple of weeks."

"Regan, what are you living on? How are you managing to eat?"

"She left me food and money. It's okay, I'm okay." Now Regan was getting alarmed at the horror on Mrs. Harris' face.

"I just have to stay home and wait," she said. "She'll be back any day now. It's okay, really." She stood up. "I gotta go now, thanks for listening."

"Regan, stop. I have to report this. You can't live on your own. I can't just let you go without knowing if you'll be okay."

"No," Regan said. "No, Mrs. Harris. Please. Really, I'm fine. They'll take me away from my mom, no, don't say anything. Please!"

The tears did start now. She couldn't seem to blink them back.

Mrs. Harris studied her. "Okay," she said. "I'll get my coat. I'm going to drive you home and see your situation. But Regan, I can't break the law, or I'll lose my job. And the law says I should report this immediately."

Regan shrank into her chair. She'd made a mistake, that was for sure. Now what was she going to do?

When she and Mrs. Harris got to the apartment, Regan unlocked the door and they both went inside. She was shocked herself to see how dusty and untidy the apartment looked. She hadn't really noticed before. There were dirty dishes in the sink, and she hadn't taken the garbage out in a while. A yellow envelope lay on the floor. She picked it up and tore it open. A notice that the electricity hadn't been paid. Of course. She crumpled it and stuffed it in her jacket pocket.

"See, there's food," Regan said, opening the fridge door and shutting it again almost immediately. There was a roll of mouldy bagels and some out-of-date yogurt.

"Regan, I have to go home and feed my kids. Why don't you come stay overnight with me? And tomorrow we'll figure out what to do. We'll talk to Social Services and they'll be able to help you."

"No, no, I have to stay here," Regan said. "Mom might come. She won't know where I am. And they'll take me away from her."

"Look, we'll leave her a note. And they won't take you away. They will help you, keep you safe, make sure you have enough to eat."

"I can't," Regan said. "I just can't."

Mrs. Harris sighed. "Yes, you can. I'll leave my phone number on the note. Regan, I can't just leave you here. You have no food. You're all by yourself. It's not good. It's really, really not safe. Look, it's just for tonight. Tomorrow, we'll figure out what to do."

Reluctantly, Regan followed her outside, got in the car, and stared moodily out the window as they drove across the city and pulled up in front of a new-looking white house on a street crowded with cars and lined with enormous trees. Regan followed Mrs. Harris into the house. Two children came running, followed by an older dark woman, who after greeting Mrs. Harris, put on a coat and hat.

"Jeremy, five, Olivia, four," Mrs. Harris announced. "And this is Camille, our nanny. Now, Regan, I am going to make us some snacks and we'll sit here and have a nice visit until my husband gets home and then we'll all have dinner together." She poured some chips into a bowl, put out some cartons of dip and poured lemonade into glasses. The two children snuck shy glances at Regan and giggled. Regan fidgeted in her chair and ate two potato chips, then downed her drink because she was so thirsty. She felt dirty. Her scalp crawled. She wondered if wherever she sat in this clean, lighted room, she left a film of dirt.

Finally, Mrs. Harris shooed them all off to watch TV while she made dinner. Regan perched on the edge of the couch and watched the Simpsons. She wanted to throw a rock through the TV, and then stand up and leave. But she didn't. She twisted her fingers tightly together. Finally, dinner was ready. Regan washed her hands in the bathroom, then sat at the table, and picked at her fried chicken and salad. She ate a piece of bread and butter, asked to be excused and flopped down in front of the TV again. She thought about simply tiptoeing to the back door and leaving but she didn't do that either.

Eventually, Mrs. Harris showed her a room to sleep in with its own bathroom, and handed her a pair of pajamas and a toothbrush. She suggested Regan might like to have a shower in a voice that meant Regan really needed to have a shower. After Regan had a very long, very hot shower, she brushed her teeth, put on the pajamas and got into bed. She lay very still, staring at the wall. Finally, she dozed off but every small noise jerked her awake. Then she lay still until she dozed off again.

As soon as a thin grey light began to seep in the window, she got up, got dressed, grabbed her backpack and headed down the hall to the back door. She left the pajamas folded on the bed.

Her feet made no sound on the carpet. She unlocked the

door and eased it open, slid outside, put on her shoes, and headed out the gate. She took deep breaths of the cold morning air. The buses weren't running yet; no matter, she'd become a jogger. She trotted down the sidewalk, heading for downtown and its familiar streets. Plans, thoughts, ideas whirled through her head.

It took her almost an hour to reach the downtown area. By now, the streets were full of traffic. She headed for the corner where Mike usually hung out, busking. She found him, drinking coffee across the street from his usual spot, sitting on a bench in a small park.

"Queenie," he said as soon as he saw her. "I been looking for you. I might know something. Or I might have heard something. Or something."

She flopped down beside him, grabbed his coffee, took a gulp. "I ran away," she said. "I gotta find another place to stay. Mrs. Harris, my teacher, is going to call the cops for sure. Can you take me back to that tent place? Do you think it would be cool to stay there?"

Mike stared at her. "Did you hear what I said? I heard something, maybe about your mom."

"What, what?"

"Like, maybe nothing. I don't know. Listen, you know I stay around here and there, you know, with guys, anyone who'll give me a place to hang out for a bit."

"Yeah, I know, I know. What?"

A cop car crawled by down the street outside the park.

Regan hid her face in Mike's shoulder. "Crap, cops."

"It's okay, they're gone. Listen, I was at that big hotel last night, at a party." He paused.

"Two people were talking, a guy and some woman. I dunno if this means anything. He was telling her about this great idea for making a lot of money fast. That's what your mom was talking about, right?"

"Yeah, she said it would only be a few days, she'd come back with some money. We'd go shopping and have a party, just the two of us. She seemed so happy."

"And then she went off with some guy, yeah? What was his name again?"

"Clayton or something like that."

"Well, that was this guy's name. What if he's the same guy?"

They were both silent for a moment.

"I guess it is kind of a stretch," Mike said.

"It might just be a coincidence, but I think I should talk to him anyway," Regan said. "Do you know where he is?"

"Yeah, he told the woman to come see him at the hotel in the morning. I remember the room number. He looked like some rich dude. It costs a lot of money to stay in that place. Big hotel down by the water."

"Let's go," Regan said. She took a final sip of the coffee, put the cup in a trash container.

"Queenie bee, I say cops."

"No. My mom doesn't trust cops."

Mike sighed. Neither of them said a word as they walked down the street. Mike's corkscrew curls bounced on his head.

When they reached the hotel, they walked in through the heavy glass doors and waited until an empty elevator dinged to a stop in front of them.

"You need a card for the elevator," Regan said.

"Oh, yeah?" he said and pulled one out of his pocket. "Courtesy of last night's party."

"What floor?"

"Eleven."

They rode up in silence, got off the elevator, walked slowly down the hall and stood in front of the door.

"You knock."

"No, you."

But while they stood there, the door opened and a man appeared.

"Who are you?" he said. His belly bulged over his belt and his eyes were narrow slits. His hair hung in a grey ponytail down his back.

"Are you Clayton?" Regan asked.

"Yeah, who in the heck are you?"

"I think you know my mom, Joanie Anderson. I'm her daughter, Regan."

"Joanie? Oh yeah, that was quite a while back. She never said nothing about a daughter."

"Look, I'm searching for her. She didn't come home and I need to find her. Where is she? I've been waiting and waiting for her to come home. I don't have any food and they're going to turn the power off and take me away to some group home and I need to find her."

"Whoa, hold on. I don't know anything," the man said. His face closed up tight. "I didn't even know she had a kid. We went to a party, had a few laughs, I hired her, paid her, she left, and that was it."

"What about the money? She said she was going to make a lot of money?"

The man sighed. "Look, I run high stakes poker games, okay. Joanie, your mom, she seemed smart, seemed able to take care of herself. I needed someone to manage stuff, you know, serve drinks, food, keep track of stuff, keep the men laughing. You know. Well, I guess you probably don't. Anyway, she did a good job, I paid her, but she met some guy, some sleazeball, and went off with him. I don't where she went. Sorry girlie, but I'm in a hurry here."

"What was the name of the sleazeball?" Mike asked.

"What?"

"A name, we need a name. Where was he from? How do we find him?"

"You kids think this is some kind of game? You playing cops and robbers here? Get outta my way. Go call the cops; they do this for real."

"His name," Mike said again.

Clayton looked at Mike. "You were at the party last night, weren't you?"

"Yep, that was me."

The man sighed. He went back in the room, turned to a laptop, fired it up, and hit some keys. A printer spit out a piece of paper.

"Here, and don't mention you got this from me. Now get out of here."

In the elevator, they looked at the paper; it had a name, George Miller, with an address, a phone number, and an email.

"Look, Queenie, I've got to make some money today or I'm not going to eat. How about I go juggle for a couple of hours, then we'll go find this guy."

"But Mike, I can't go home. If the cops pick me up, they'll take me away. At least we know now that Mom is somewhere; maybe she is with this guy. Maybe she has amnesia. Maybe he kidnapped her. There's got to be some reason why she didn't come home."

"Look, don't go over there by yourself, whatever you do."

"I'll just go look."

"Okay. Whatever."

"Mike, can you give me some bus fare?"

"I told you I'm busted. Go panhandle for it."

"I can't."

But he had turned away and was heading down the street. Regan's stomach hurt. She sat on a bus bench, her head in her hands. Finally it had stopped raining. The clouds had opened, the sky cleared, the sun was hot on her head. She pulled her backpack onto her lap, held onto it, rocking back and forth, her eyes closed.

"Hey, dear," said a voice by her ear. "You hungry? You need anything?"

She looked up. An older lady with her hair in a long grey braid was standing beside her. She was leaning on a cane. She was wearing a long black coat with silver threads running through it that looked expensive.

"Yes," Regan said. "I'm very hungry."

"Here, then, dear. I hope this helps." The lady handed her a twenty-dollar bill and limped off down the street. She was shaking her head.

Regan studied the twenty dollars as if she had never seen money before. She turned it over, looked at both sides; she tried to decide whether to go buy a loaf of bread and some cheese and milk or just go get a hamburger. In the end, the hamburger won. It was just faster. She walked to McDonald's, ordered a burger and gulped it down.

Then she got on a bus and followed the bus driver's directions on how to get to the address on the piece of paper.

Eventually, she made it to the address. It was a tall, blue and white apartment building with big balconies and a two-storey penthouse. It looked really expensive. What would her mother be doing in such a place? She walked up and down the street and around the block, thinking. There was no place for her to sit and watch the door of the building without looking foolishly conspicuous, not without a car. Her stomach was clenched around the food she had eaten earlier and her throat hurt. It was hard to swallow, her throat was so dry.

Finally, she stepped up to the door of the building and punched in the number for the apartment. A woman's voice answered.

"Delivery for Anderson," she said, trying to sound like a bored delivery person. The buzzer sounded and she yanked the door open, ran inside and ran to the elevator before she could lose her nerve. She punched 5 and when the elevator doors opened, marched to number 510. Her throat was still too dry to speak and she cleared it.

A woman opened the door to her knock. The woman had slicked-back black hair pulled into a knot, red lipstick, a skin-tight green dress, and shiny black shoes with high heels.

"Hi," Regan said. "I'm looking for Joanie Anderson?"

"I thought you were a delivery," said the woman. "What do you want?"

"I'm looking for Joanie Anderson. She's my mom and she's gone missing. This is the address I have for her."

"Well, aren't you the bright little chicken. Where did you come from, eh?" The woman leaned against the door. "Sorry, no Joanie Anderson here. Never heard of her. Maybe you want to come in, have a drink, watch TV or something."

"No thanks," said Regan. "Do you have any way I can contact my mom?"

The woman's eyes narrowed. "Oh, I really think you should come in," she said. "I really think we need to have a chat. George," she called over her shoulder. "George, come and see this."

A man appeared over her shoulder, a man with blond hair wearing a sleek grey suit.

"Look at this little chicken that just wandered in off the street. Don't you think we should invite her in?"

"No thanks," said Regan, "I'm just looking for my mom, Joanie Anderson."

"Not here," the man said. "She took off, took a big pile of

money with her, money that didn't belong to her. You see her, you tell her old George is looking for her, yes he is, and he wants his money. C'mon in, girlie, you and me should talk."

"No," said Regan but George grabbed her arm.

"Get inside," George snarled. "Maybe if Mommy knows you're here, she'll play nice."

But the minute George grabbed her arm, Regan reacted. It was as if Sifu's voice was playing in her head. "Block, grab, punch, kick." Her foot connected with the man's kneecap.

George screamed a long howl of pain and Regan raced for the elevator. Frantically she pushed the buttons. Nothing happened and she scooted for the red exit sign that she knew would be a staircase, yanked open the heavy metal door, and then slid and ran down the five flights of stairs, out the door, and onto the street. She bent over gasping for air and then headed towards the corner at a fast trot, trying to look like a jogger, out to the main street and a bus stop. But at the bus stop, she couldn't sit still. Instead, she headed down the street at a fast walk. Suddenly, she spotted a black van with two men in it that had slowed down. One of the men stared at her.

Not good. There wasn't a store or a coffee shop she could get into, just blocks of houses and apartment buildings. She ducked into a path between some bushes, beside an apartment building and ran out the back into an alley, crossed it and into another alley, then out through a yard and into a different street. She kept ducking in and out of alleys and streets until she thought perhaps she had thrown them off the track.

But now she couldn't go home and she couldn't stay on the street either. At a fast trot, she headed for the bridge that Mike had shown her but had to keep stopping, doubling over with a stitch in her side. Nervously, she watched over her shoulder for the black van or cars with two men, but nothing appeared. When she finally reached the bridge, it was late afternoon. She was cold and hungry. The hamburger she had eaten earlier seemed a long time ago. She scrambled down the side, through the alleyway of blackberry thorns, and into the clearing.

As before, a fire was burning and people were sitting around it. All conversation stopped and everyone's eyes turned to her when she burst into the clearing.

She hesitated and then came forward to the fire.

"I got no place to go," she said. "I came here with Mike yesterday. I just need a place to hide for a bit."

No one said anything. Then one of the older men grunted. "Sit down, no one will find you here. We're all running from something, ourselves, mostly." He cackled, a high gleeful sound. She sat on the ground next to the fire. The warmth felt good on her face and hands.

Someone came out of one of the tents and into the firelight. Regan could see it was the large woman she had seen before; she was wearing several long skirts, a scarf tied on her head, and big men's boots with no laces. She stared at Regan.

"You look half starved," the woman said. "Zack, get the poor kid some food."

Zack handed Regan a bowl of something with rice and meat and beans in it. "Here kid, eat up," he mumbled without looking at her.

It tasted fantastic. She finished the bowl and without a word, the woman took it from her and refilled it, then poured her a mug of steaming mint tea as well.

The woman settled heavily onto a log next to Regan. "Kid, don't get old," she said. "It really sucks."

Regan nodded, her mouth too full of food to speak. No one said anything for a while. Regan finished her food and set the bowl on the ground. She watched the fire while the strange events of the day played themselves over in her head. After a while, she realized she had been dozing. A thin misty rain started to fall.

"C'mon kid, you can sleep in my tent. I got a spare sleeping bag." Regan nodded, grateful for any shelter. The woman went ahead of her, grunted as she unearthed a sleeping bag and a thin blue foamie. Regan crawled into the musty sleeping bag and fell asleep almost immediately.

She woke in the middle of the night. Rain spattered on the tent; the bulk of the fat woman beside her rose and fell as she snored in her sleep. Outside, waves rattled the gravel on the beach of the channel under the bridge, and far away, a foghorn sounded in the bay. The events of the day began to play themselves over and over in her head. She pulled her knees up and locked her arms around them but fear kept churning in her belly. Her knees hurt. She pushed her legs straight and turned over, trying to get comfortable.

The big woman stopped snoring, sighed and muttered sleepily, "Kid, everything looks worse in the middle of the night. My shrink told me that and he was right. Something about us once being hunted by sabre-toothed tigers or some such. Whatever it is, we'll deal with it in the morning. Okay?"

Overhead on the bridge, the steady rustle of car tires sounded like the wind blowing. Regan turned over so her back was to the woman. She could feel the woman's body heat radiating towards her. She sighed deeply and drifted back to sleep.

Chapter Four

WHEN REGAN WOKE in the morning, she had no idea where she was. She stared at the glowing blue fabric of the tent over her head, then over at the woman sleeping beside her. Then it flooded back, the previous day, the man and woman in the apartment, the black van and two men who might have been looking for her.

The woman opened her eyes, sighed deeply. "Getting up is always the hardest part of the day," she said and laughed. She threw back her sleeping bag, rolled over, got on her hands and knees, grabbed a stick that was lying beside her sleeping mat, and hoisted herself to her feet.

"Hey kid, I'm Ramona, what's your name?"

"I'm Regan, Regan Anderson."

"You looked pretty scared when you wandered in here yesterday. Look, let me get the coffee on and we can talk. You can tell me whatever you want. Everyone here has a story of some kind. We don't worry too much about whether it's true or not." She laughed, a big rolling laugh that seemed to come right out of her belly.

The woman seemed so friendly that Regan began to relax. She, too, rolled out of the musty sleeping bag, stood up, and ducked out of the tent after Ramona.

"Bathroom's over there," said Ramona, pointing at some bushes. Regan saw there was a well-beaten path that led to a hole in the ground and a plank balanced over it. The hole stank.

When she came back, Ramona was pouring water from a blue tub into a kettle. She hung the kettle on a hook suspended over the firepit, then moving quickly, grabbed an axe, pulled some wood out from under a tarp, chopped some kindling off a block of wood, poured something out of a plastic jug onto the kindling and touched a match to it. Flames leapt up and covered the wood. The woman next filled a pot with water, dumped oatmeal into it, put a lid on it, and balanced it on two rocks next to the flames.

Other people were stirring now. One man, then another, came to the fire. Soon there were five men, plus Ramona, standing around the fire. The kettle shot steam from its spout, and Ramona grabbed a towel, wrapped it around the kettle's handle, and poured hot water through a filter full of coffee grounds into a big thermos jug.

"Come and get it," she said. The men shuffled over to the table, which also held a plastic washbasin, a bunch of mugs, various plastic bags and bowls, a grey plastic tub, and some towels.

As the men came back to the fire, Ramona introduced them, one by one. "Zack, Hector, Rafe, Limpy, and Seb."

She poured Regan a cup of coffee, added a spoonful of sugar and handed it to her. Regan didn't really like coffee but she took it and sipped the bitter-sweet, slightly muddy drink. She shivered and Ramona ducked back into the tent and came out with a brown shawl that she wrapped around Regan's shoulders. The morning was grey and a thin mist hung in the air.

For a while there was silence around the fire. Regan looked around the camp. She had never been camping. Her grandmother had liked to take a picnic lunch to the park once in a while. That was about it. But this place looked organized. There was even a big garbage can at the end of the driftwood plank table.

"How long have you—um—all lived here?" she asked.

Ramona shrugged. "Couple of months. Cops will find us one of these days and run us off. Or the rain will come." The others nodded.

"We're all binners," she told Regan. "We live good in the summer off the bottles and stuff we find, but now it's fall, and we won't be able to stay here when winter really sets in. Can't keep a fire going, can't ever get warm or dry. Winters are hard.

Most of us won't go in shelters. We can get dry there, spend the days, but the nights aren't good. If it don't get too cold, well, then we make out here for a while longer. But if she snows . . . whoo, look out. So people come and go here. And I don't let no bad behaviour happen in my camp."

The others nodded. There was Hector, who was small and dark and seemed nervous, kept jerking and twitching his shoulders, Rafe, who was enormous, and Limpy, who did limp, but was younger than the rest and quite good-looking. Zack looked like the oldest of the bunch. He had a kind face. Seb wouldn't look at her, just kept his eyes on the ground.

"Well, c'mon you guys, get yourselves some breakfast. We're runnin' outta beans and snacks. Today, you're gonna have to get out there and bring home something to eat." The men nodded. Ramona lifted the lid on the pot of oatmeal and stirred. "Sugar, no milk left," she said. The men helped themselves to oatmeal, and Ramona served Regan a bowl. When the men finished, they each carried their empty bowl to the dishpan and set it in there along with their empty cups.

"So what the heck is someone thinking, leave a little girl like you on your own? You got no one to look after you? What is this crazy world coming to?" asked Zack as he came back to the fire. He shook his head. Zack was elderly with grey hair, a stringy beard, and dark brown skin. When he smiled, Regan could see he didn't have teeth, just brown stubs.

"I'm not that young," Regan said, but the others were nodding in agreement.

They all looked at her. "We don't pry here," said Ramona. "You can tell us or not. It's up to you. You can stay here if you want, but if there's people looking for you, parents, cops, anyone else, that would be good to know."

Regan looked around the circle of faces. She sighed. "My mom's gone missing." I went to some dude's apartment building yesterday and he said my mom had stolen his money. He tried to grab me and pull me into his place but I kicked him and ran away. And then some guys in a van were following me. So I came here."

They nodded. "Well, that sucks," said Limpy. He shook his head. "No mom, that means if they catch you, they'll bang you up in a group home somewhere. Man, I hate those places. Ran away so many times, they finally gave up. Now I'm a junkie drunk but even that's better than being in one of them joints."

Zack nodded. "I been hearing stories of girls going missing. Bad stuff goin' on, bad stuff. Always bad stuff."

Regan felt her face grow hot. "My mom is great," she said. "She used to work in Seven-Eleven. She looks after me really well. We got a nice place. We get along. She said she'd only be gone a couple of days. She left me food and money. Now it's been three weeks. I think she must have been kidnapped, or maybe she's hiding from this guy. I've got to find her. I'm out of food and now these men are looking for me."

They all nodded. "Nice to have a mom like that," said Zack. "She sounds great. Listen kid, we can ask around. The street is one big gossip grapevine. Stay here. Cops don't come down here, and if they do, we'll hear them coming and we'll get you out of here."

"Thanks," Regan said. "I've been pretty scared."

"I been wandering these streets way too long," said Zack. "They ain't no place for kids. I know there's kids out there and it's wrong, just plain wrong. What kinda people can't care for their own damn kids? Well come on, you lazy busters, let's go on the big hunt."

They got to their feet and filed out of the clearing. Regan and Ramona sat together. The mist had cleared and the sun was shining on the distant harbour. Small brown birds hopped and flitted through the brush around the camp. It was very quiet apart from the endless swish of traffic overhead.

"Hey, look up," Ramona said, pointing. Regan looked where Ramona was pointing. "See, it's an eagle. See all them gulls and ravens circling around, yelling at him. Old eagle just ignores them. He knows his own strength."

Regan watched the eagle circling over the sun-bright water. Eventually, it circled high into the sky where she could no longer see it.

"It's so nice here," Regan said.

"Yes, it is," said Ramona. "But I have to stay here. If I go downtown, in all that traffic, I start to lose it." She sighed deeply. "I don't hear the voices when I'm here."

"My friend Annie hears voices too."

"Yeah, I know Annie. She's tougher than I am. She can

handle the noise. But we can't stay here in the winter. It's just too hard."

"Where will you go?"

"The hospital, jail, shelters, whatever." Ramona shrugged. "I don't want to think about it right now. So tell me about your mom? Don't you have other family? Do you have any idea where your mom would have gone?"

"I have a grandma," Regan said. "She's in Nicola Lake. We used to live with her and then she and my mom had a fight. She was my dad's mom. She was nice, I liked her."

"Can't you call her?"

"I don't have a phone. Mom has a cell phone but she took it with her."

"Do you know your grandma's number?"

Regan wrinkled her forehead. "No, I can't remember it. Her name is Nora Anderson though."

"Okay, hang on. I'll get my phone."

Ramona ducked into the tent, and came out, not only with a phone but a small computer.

"Wow," Regan said.

"Yeah, you can get anything cheap these days if you know where to go and who to ask. Zack brought these back one day—he traded for them, don't know what, don't want to know. All we had to do was buy a phone card—and look, the computer has this weird gizmo on it, so somehow we keep getting internet. Someone must be paying for it, don't know who. Okay, now look for your grandma's phone number."

Regan took the computer into the shade of the tent so she could see the screen. She noticed there was hardly any battery left. "How do you plug it in?" she asked.

"Gotta take it up to a coffee shop somewhere."

Regan found the Nicola Lake phone book online, and there was her grandmother's name. Why hadn't she thought of this before? Maybe her mom was hiding out in Nicola Lake? But then why hadn't she gotten a message to Regan somehow? It still didn't make any sense.

With trembling hands, she punched in her grandmother's phone number.

"Hello," said a quavering voice. Even though it had been a few years, Regan recognized the voice as her grandmother's. She had been kind and Regan had never understood why her mom had gotten mad at her grandmother. She had only been two when her dad was killed. She didn't remember him at all, but she remembered the sound of her grandma's crying seeping through the thin bedroom walls at night. And she remembered the sounds of her mother and her grandmother arguing. It had something to do with money. That was all she knew.

"Grandma, it's me, Regan."

"Who? Oh, Regan, honey, so good to hear from you. What a surprise. Are you okay?"

"Yes, I'm fine." Now Regan hesitated. What could she say that wouldn't make her grandmother suspicious? "Grandma, did my mom call you?"

"Your mom? No, I haven't heard from her and I don't expect to. She made that pretty clear when you two left. Regan, it's been so long. I have missed you so much." Her grandmother's voice was shaky. She sounded really old. But even so, Regan could hear the longing in her grandmother's voice. Why had they left? And why hadn't her mother ever let Regan go back for a visit?

"I miss you too, Grandma."

"Why are you asking about your mom?"

"Oh, no reason. She might need to go away for a while. She asked me if I would like to go visit you."

"Oh, Regan, I'd love to see you so much. It has been so long. Listen, if I sent you a bus ticket, do you think your mom would really let you come visit?"

"I dunno, maybe."

"Oh Regan, I would be so glad to see you. I bet you look just like your dad."

"I don't know if I do or not."

"Okay, that's what I am going to do, I am going to run down to the bus station right away and buy a ticket and put it in the mail. You can use it any time. Do you still live on Alexander Street?"

"Yeah."

"Then I have your address. At least your mom sent me that. Oh, I am so excited. Let me know when you are coming. I'll make all your favourite foods."

"Okay, Grandma."

"Oh, Regan, I love you sweetie, oh I am so excited."

"Okay, Grandma, listen, gotta go, okay. Love you too."

Regan clicked the phone off and handed it to Ramona. Then, for the second time in three days, she burst into tears.

"Oh, poor Grandma. She sounded so lonely. I hope she's okay."

"Maybe she's just worried about you."

"I haven't seen her for so long. Maybe I should go stay with her for a bit?"

"Well, it would solve a bunch of problems," Ramona said. "You wouldn't have to worry about the welfare locking you up, and you'd have someone to feed you and look after you. Then when your mom shows up, you could go back with her. Maybe your mom and your grandma could make up."

"But I need to stay here. I want to find my mom! What if something has happened to her? What if she's hurt or kidnapped. I've got to find her."

"Look, honey, you have got to at least report her missing. I'd go with you to the cop house but that would make the voices start. I'm scared to go there. Then they might lock me up. If they did, this camp would fall apart. These guys need me to keep them fed and clean, and in return, they buy the groceries, booze sometimes, whatever."

"How do you get clean?" Regan asked cautiously. She had noticed—but didn't want to say anything—the dark mat of dirt in the creases of Ramona's neck, the fact that her long skirt and heavy quilted man's shirt were stained with grease and food.

"Yeah, that's a problem." Ramona sighed heavily. "We get

water from the gas station up the hill but it's heavy and there's never enough for everything. Sometimes, if I'm feeling good, I make it all the way up the hill to the laundromat, but I can only handle it for so long and then I gotta leave. Mostly we just live dirty."

"There's still hot water at my place. The power is going to get turned off but I think the hot water goes in all the apartments so I can have a shower. Listen, Ramona, if I go home and change and get some clean clothes, can I come back here tonight? And I'll think about going to the cops but I can't go by myself. I need a grown-up to go with me and pretend I am staying with them, so the cops don't lock me up."

"Sure, kid, whatever. You got any money?"

"A bit."

"Okay, that's good, cause you gotta chip in if you're gonna stay. We got to eat and we got to have smokes and stuff. Everybody who stays here helps out. That's the rule."

"Okay, sure." She still had fifteen bucks left from the twenty the woman had given her. She had planned to hang onto it but she felt guilty eating the camp food and not contributing. She fished it out of her pocket and handed it to Ramona but kept back the change, enough for bus fare.

"Okay, Ramona, thanks for everything. See you later."

Regan grabbed her backpack, headed back out through the bush and up the bank to the bridge. She looked around carefully, and once she was on the bridge, she started to jog with her head down. She jogged across to the other side, where she dodged down side streets and alleys, still running, until she got to her apartment building. She stood in the alley, watching, but there was no sign of a black van, or anyone watching the building.

She unlocked the front door, ran up the stairs to the second floor and stopped. The door to her apartment had been kicked in. There was no noise. She went very cautiously in the door. The apartment was silent, a few things had been moved but as far as she could tell, nothing had been taken. Her mother's mattress had been turned over, and the dresser drawers had been opened and everything dumped on the floor.

Regan started to shake. This was too much. She went into her own room. Nothing seemed to have been moved. Still shaking, she pulled her backpack off her shoulders, took out the schoolbooks, crammed in some underwear, some t-shirts, a sweater, socks, and a knitted hat. None of it was really clean but it was cleaner than the clothes she had slept in last night. Then she stood up and started to leave. But standing in the door of the apartment were two tall cops, a man and a woman. And they were not looking friendly.

"What's going on here?" said the tallest one, a man. He was young and had a thin narrow face and bright blue eyes. "We got a complaint from the neighbours that someone was smashing things. Care to tell us about that?"

"Um, I just got here," said Regan. "I live here. I just found the apartment like this."

"So where's your mom?"

"She's at work."

"And where would that be? Shouldn't you be in school? Where were you last night if you just got here now?"

"I was staying with a friend. I just came home to change my clothes."

"Hmm," said the cop. "Mind if we look around?" He didn't wait for her answer. Both cops came in, looked through the kitchen, the living room, the bedrooms, looked in the fridge, looked in dresser drawers.

"So, kid, how do we get a hold of your mom?"

"She works at Seven-Eleven on Cambie. Look, I've got to get back to school."

"Why don't you come with us, we'll go find your mom, talk to the landlord, clear this whole thing up. C'mon kid."

The female cop grabbed her arm and Regan half walked and was half dragged downstairs, where she was shoved into the back of the police cruiser. Once they arrived, she sat inside, staring out of the window, while the male cop went inside Seven-Eleven and talked to the clerks there. She could see them shaking their heads.

The cop came back out and got in the cruiser.

"So, kid, they say your mom hasn't been around in a while, say two, three weeks. So care to tell us where she is? And by the way, your teacher called to tell us you were on the streets. Not a good place for you to be hanging out, kid."

Regan said nothing, just stared out the window. The two cops looked at each other, shrugged. They drove to the big police station, pulled her out of the car, grabbed her arm and took her into the station, where they sat her in a small bare room. The female cop came in and sat down.

"So Regan, my name is Brenda Silsbie. Now, you got anyone we can call to come and look after you?" Brenda asked.

"No."

"Care to tell us how you've been coping on your own for three weeks?"

"My mom will be back soon. I'm fine. Just let me go home."

"Who kicked in the door?"

"I don't know. I wasn't there."

"Where were you?"

"At a friend's."

"What friend? Can you give us a name and address?"

"I can't tell you, I promised I wouldn't."

"Well, you're not making our job any easier, that's for sure. So apparently your teacher, a Mrs. Harris, has also reported your mom missing. You're going to have to go to a group home until we can find your mom, but stay there, please. We don't want to have to do this again. So now, let's talk about your mom. When did you see her last?"

Regan sighed. "September 21st. She said she was just going somewhere for a couple of days. She left some money and some food. But I got worried and went to look for her and I found this guy, up on 41st, who said she might have taken some money. So I've been looking around and trying to figure out how to find her."

The cop actually smiled. "Well, that's supposed to be our job. Why didn't you come to us?"

"Because you would take me away from my mom and she's a really good mom."

"Good moms don't leave their kids alone and take off with someone."

"She's not like that."

"You know, Regan, a lot of women go missing down here. It's not a good part of town for women and kids."

"I don't mind it. I know how to look after myself."

"You shouldn't have to look after yourself. You're a kid. You might think that you're smart but it's still darned dangerous. I see kids like you in trouble all the time. Have you and your mom ever thought of moving somewhere else?"

"We're going to move as soon as she gets some money."

"So, what does your mom do for a living?"

"She works at Seven-Eleven. You went there."

"And that's how she supports herself?"

"Yeah."

"And what do you do?"

"What do you mean?"

"How do you support yourself? Without your mother around?"

"I don't work," Regan said. "I go to school."

"Not lately. Your teachers tell us you've been away a lot. What have you been up to? You've got to be making money somehow. You can't be living on nothing."

"I was looking for my mother. And I didn't have any clean clothes." That last remark sounded stupid and Regan knew it sounded stupid, but it was the truth. She couldn't stand to go to school in dirty clothes and have the other kids think she didn't even know how to keep clean.

"Okay, sure, whatever you say. But you know, if you've been lying to us, we'll figure it out pretty quick. Right now, I need to know whatever you can tell us about where you think your mom got to and then we'll see what we can do. Here, write down the name and address of this guy you say you talked to." Brenda handed her a piece of paper and Regan wrote down what little she knew. The cop didn't seem very interested. She obviously didn't believe Regan's story.

Then Regan waited in the small room by herself for the social worker to show up and take her to a group home somewhere in the city.

Chapter Five

⬷

ZACK LOOKED AT HER and laughed as she puffed into camp, slid her backpack onto the ground, and slumped onto a log.

"Got out of lock-up, did you? Hope no one is chasing you." He cackled, a high-pitched cackle-like a crazy crow. "Well, you sure didn't stay too long. Good for you, Regan. Them places aren't healthy."

"Well, they tried to be nice," Regan said. "But it was so noisy. Everyone was supposed to be in their rooms and in bed by nine o'clock, but people were running around all night. Still, I got a shower and got my clothes cleaned. And the cops are sort of looking for my mom. Maybe. So, I guess it all turned out okay."

She yawned and looked around the camp. She hadn't slept

the night before. The social worker that had picked her up at the police station had come to talk to her this morning and had driven her to school. She had walked in the front door of the school and out the back, dodged down alleyways and then jogged over the bridge until she got back to the camp under the bridge.

Ramona and Zack were there, sitting in the sun, both smoking cigarettes. No one else was around.

"I went in the front of the school and out the back," Regan said. "I don't think anyone noticed."

Zack grunted.

"The group home will notify the social worker when you don't come and they'll notify the police, but no one will do nothing. I should know. I grew up in them places. They'd put me in a foster home; I'd run away. They'd stick me in a group home; I'd run away. All I wanted to do was go home but they wouldn't send me there."

"Where was your home?" Regan asked.

"I was born in a little town called Bella Coola, right on the ocean. Beautiful place. I go to the library and look at pictures sometimes. Always wanted to go back there."

"Why didn't you?" Regan asked.

"Dunno really. A few times, I almost did. But I left when I was a kid. Don't really know anyone there now. My mom got killed in an accident. Fishing boat. Turned over in a storm. Social workers shipped me down here. Never left. Guess I'm used to it now."

"But why don't you go back if you miss it?"

"Ain't you the nosy one?" Zack said. But he didn't look angry, just very sad.

"Sorry, Zack," Regan said. "Ramona told me you guys don't like a lot of questions."

"Ahh, it's okay, kid. I just never talk about it. I guess I've missed my mom every day since then. Some days I think maybe I should just die and get it over with, go see her. Maybe she's waiting for me, eh? But then I look around and figure I'll stay here a little longer."

But Regan could tell that Zack was still upset. He shifted on his log chair, threw his cigarette in the fire, tore another one from the pack and lit it. Finally he said, "Ramona, I got to get out of here. Get going, do something." A muscle twitched on the side of his face. He took off his hat, scratched his head, put his hat back on, stood up, sat down, stood up again. Then he left the camp without a word.

Regan watched him go. "Sorry, Ramona, I guess I should have been quiet."

"It's not your fault, Regan. Doesn't take much to upset Zack. Don't worry about it."

They sat together awhile longer in the sun without saying anything.

"Regan, can you take that little computer up to a coffee shop, plug it in for a bit? I'll give you some money so you can eat something while you're there."

"Sure," Regan said.

Ramona handed her the computer and a five-dollar bill.

Regan slid the computer into her backpack, and headed back up the hill. She yawned. She hadn't slept much the past couple of nights. She could use another hot shower, and then a whole night's sleep in a soft bed, a bed with many covers and clean sheets. And she could wear pajamas again. Once her mom had bought her red pajamas with white teddy bears on them. She had loved those pajamas. She wore them out and finally her mom threw them away. Her mom did some wonderful things sometimes. And then she did stupid things too.

Regan stopped on the sidewalk, suddenly struck by that thought. She'd always kind of taken her mom for granted. Her mom was her mom, red-haired, brown eyes, often tired. She usually stayed in bed in the morning while Regan got herself off to school. Her mom often worked late, or she went out on a date with one of the faceless men. Her mom always made time for her on weekends, or occasionally after school. During the week they hardly saw each other, but Regan didn't mind. That's what she told herself. Her mom did the best she could. They were always short of money and her mom worked hard.

Now the words of Brenda, the police officer, came back to her. The cops seemed to think her mom was a bad mom, that her mom didn't care about her, that she'd run off. Abandoned her. It was as if everything the cop said to her had two meanings. And why had the cops asked what her mom did for a living? Did they think she was a prostitute? Regan stopped in the middle of the sidewalk.

That wasn't true. Her mom loved her, she was sure of that. And then she thought of her teacher, Mrs. Harris, of her shining clean home, full of new furniture, her two small children, her kind, gentle husband. He worked in a bank somewhere. Maybe if her dad hadn't died, they would have all been able to live like that. But no, they wouldn't have lived in the city; they would have stayed in the country, maybe in Nicola Lake. Maybe she would have had a dog, even a pony. There was a time in her life when she would have done anything to have a pony.

For a moment, she felt a flash of anger towards her mother. Then she remembered her mom laughing; she could almost hear her laughing. "Regan, you're my queen bee," she'd say. "C'mon, let's go have some fun." And they would. Even if it was only going to the park or wandering along the seawall because they couldn't afford anything else.

So maybe what she would do was go to one of her mom's favourite coffee shops, and she'd pretend she was with her mom. She'd think about her mom's voice, her laughter, and she'd order the food her mom always ordered. She grabbed the next bus downtown and headed for the coffee shop that was called "The Other Side." No one knew why it was called that. The owner was a kindly older man named Terry.

She went in, said hello to Terry, stood at the counter, ordered the breakfast bagel with avocado, and grabbed a glass of water to go with it.

She moved to the back of the room, to a small table partly

screened by the booths in front of it. She plugged in the computer Ramona had given her, went online, cruised through several of her favourite websites, and finally plugged in the name of the man who had been in the blue apartment building. A number of websites came up; one of them was for playing online poker. She read through the little bit of information that was there, and went back to eating her bagel and checking out music and movie sites. It had been a long time since she had had the freedom of the internet, clicking through from site to site. She was so involved, she forgot to pay attention to the people coming in.

And then she heard a voice that froze her in her seat. It was the same man, George Miller, and the woman who had been with him in the apartment, the woman with black hair and scarlet fingernails. They hadn't seen her, probably because she had her head down and was in the shadows at the back and they were busy ordering food, looking up at the printed menu over the counter.

Regan unplugged the computer, stuffed it in her backpack, shrugged it on, and, still keeping her head down, stood up and headed for the back door. Once outside in the alley, she began walking quickly, not running; she didn't want to draw attention to herself. But behind her she heard a voice.

"Hey, girl, get back here!" Running footsteps.

Regan took off as fast as she could, out onto the sidewalk dodging people, cutting across streets against red lights, dodging cars and buses, down another alley, the backpack slamming rhythmically against her back, *bounce, bounce*, across the middle of another block, thinking as she ran—she couldn't go back to the camp—she'd never make it across the bridge, but she needed somewhere to hide. There was a Skytrain station. Down the stairs, almost flying now, and yes, a train was in the station, she ducked into it, the doors closed and she flopped into a seat.

"You got a ticket, kid?" A green-suited attendant stood in front of her, holding out his hand.

"Oops, sorry, I was in a hurry, I must have dropped it." She made a pretense of hunting through her pockets.

"Get off at the next stop and get a ticket," the bored attendant said, and moved away.

As soon as the train pulled into the next station, Regan darted out the door, ran up the escalator, and emerged onto the street. Yes, he was there, Mike, in his usual spot, next to the small city park, busking, juggling, laughing and bantering with the one or two people watching.

Regan slid to a halt beside him and put her head down, puffing. "Mike, that dude, he's after me."

"What dude?"

"That George guy . . . I went to see him. He spotted me in the coffee shop."

"Queenie, I told you not to go there alone."

"Yeah, I know, but I had to find out what's going on. He said my mom took his money. He tried to grab me when I went to his place, I've been staying at that camp under the bridge." Her breath was slowing now. She could talk without panting. "Mike, I've got to get off the street. I need somewhere else to stay."

Mike sighed. "I'm kind of short of living space myself at the moment. Maybe you need to think of getting out of town somewhere. You got any place you could go?"

"I have a grandmother in Nicola Lake. She said she was going to send me a bus ticket. I wonder if she did?"

"Regan, babe, you're in over your head here. These are not nice men to mess with. If you got somewhere to go, then go there. You know, you're a great kid but I can't look after myself, let alone you."

"Someone broke into my mom's apartment. While I was there, the cops picked me up. They stuck me in a group home, but I didn't stay there. I went back to the camp."

"Ay, yi, Regan, this just gets worse and worse. Now you got, what, cops, welfare, dude, and who knows what else looking for you? And no sign of your mom?"

"No. Not yet, anyway."

"Okay, we're going to go check your apartment mail for that bus ticket and then if it's there, I'm putting you on the bus and if it's not, well, you'd better get back to the camp. You'll be safe there."

They headed for Regan's apartment, sticking to back alleys and side streets. Regan waited in an alley while Mike darted across the street, in the door, and checked the mailboxes just inside the front door. He came back out shaking his head.

"It's only been a couple of days," Regan said. "Maybe it will be here tomorrow. But for now, I have to hide."

"Here's bus fare," Mike said impatiently. "Look, I gotta go . . . I'll meet you at the camp under the bridge. Later, maybe. I got stuff to do." He was jigging impatiently from foot to foot, his black corkscrew hair bouncing on his head. His eyes looked strange. And then he took off at a half-run, half-walk down the street. Regan stared after him, puzzled.

Mike had been her sort-of friend since she was twelve and hanging around on street corners, trying to figure out life in this city after she and her mom had lived in a succession of small towns. They had just moved to the apartment; Regan didn't know anyone in the city and her mom was usually at work. She wandered the streets, occasionally being stared at or followed by strange looking people. She had heard about this downtown area before they moved here, that it was full of drugs, drunks, violence and crime. At first, she was too scared to go far from home, but gradually, the noise, the traffic and the constant barrage of people began to seem normal. Her explorations got longer.

One sunny Saturday afternoon, it hadn't seemed menacing at all. Regan looked in store windows, bought a smokie sausage from a street vendor, looked at necklaces, spent a couple of hours draped over a chair in a giant bookstore, reading graphic novels. She was lonely but then she knew loneliness far too well.

She had counted their moves once. She and her mother

had moved six times in one year. They had lived in a whole variety of small towns, and now they were in this big city. Regan had managed to make a friend or two in each small school she attended and she kept in touch with a few of them on Facebook. But their friendship, such as it was, faded quickly whenever she moved away.

She had met Mike a few days later, when he had been busking in his favourite spot beside the small park. Regan had sat on the wall beside the park and watched him. When he was done, and the tiny crowd had dispersed, he came over and sat down beside her.

He had light brown skin, corkscrew black curls, white teeth, a lot of earrings, and an infectious laugh. She had seen him before in this park. It seemed to be his regular spot.

"Hey kid, you look a little lost," he had said. "Just learn to juggle. Then the world is always your friend." He tossed the balls in the air and when he tried to catch them, he fell over backwards, laughing.

To him, everything seemed funny, even when it wasn't. Regan had never really figured out where he lived or if he lived anywhere. He just appeared and disappeared with some regularity and whenever she saw him, he sat beside her. The second time she met him, he invited her to go to the library with him. Since this was one of Regan's favourite places in the city, she went. Once they were inside the library, they separated, each going to their favourite section. When she went to look for him, he was gone.

Still, he seemed to like hanging out with her; he was someone she could usually count on to make her laugh, even when she was really down in the dumps. And he was usually happy to go along with her to the library or the harbour shore, her two favourite places in the city.

But now he was gone, just as suddenly. She looked at the coins in her hand. Right. The bus. Should she go to the camp? Wouldn't that be bringing danger down on them? Plus she remembered Ramona saying they knew when strangers were coming. She realized with a sudden start she had to take the charged-up computer back to them.

And there was the bus. Sighing, she stepped on board, stood near the door at the back as the bus made its way across the bridge, got off several stops too far, and then went carefully through the back alleys, and down through the brush to the camp.

They all looked up as she came out into the clearing. No one seemed surprised to see her.

Ramona looked up and laughed. "Wow, takes you a while to charge up a computer." She dipped a bowl into the pot of food simmering on the fire and handed it to Regan. Regan gulped down the hot spicy soup; she wasn't sure what was in it but she was too hungry to care.

After she rinsed the bowl, she huddled on a log close to the fire. The heat felt good on her face and her hands but her back was freezing. Ramona brought a quilt and draped it over her. There was silence except for the crackling and spitting from the salt-laden driftwood, and the wind in the thick walls of brush around the campsite.

"Tough day?" said Zack, coming into the firelight with another armload of wood.

"Yeah," said Regan. She wasn't sure what to say. She didn't want them to think anyone was chasing her. They might ask her to leave, or they might be angry if she brought trouble to the camp.

"We've all had a few of those." He threw down the wood, and then knelt and placed a few pieces carefully on the fire. "Gotta go farther and farther for wood. Winter high tides will bring in a new supply, but she's gettin' scarce for now."

"Here's the computer," Regan said to Ramona, easing it out of her backpack. "Thanks, it was handy."

"Do you need it?" Ramona asked. "Can you use it?"

"Well, sure . . ."

"Then keep it, we can get another one if we need to. I actually don't like having them around. The electricity is hard on my brain. They got voices inside them, those boxes. In fact, put it back in the backpack and maybe hide it somewhere."

"Okay," Regan said. "Gee, thanks, I mean, that's amazing. My own computer. Wow."

"Ahh, it's just stuff. We weren't really using it. What for? Besides, there's lots of stuff around . . . way too much. It's money that's hard to come by."

There were nods around the campfire from the other men.

"Funny, we can get all the stolen electronic crap in the world if we want but we got no use for it. Instead we make money out of garbage," said Hector and laughed. Rafe, Limpy, and Seb all nodded.

"Darned fine work we do," said Rafe. "Clean up the city, keep the recycling flowing." Rafe had a round red face, broad shoulders under his torn plaid shirt, and he wore a tattered grey toque on his head. He spread his feet towards the fire. He was wearing almost new expensive running shoes on his enormous feet. He saw Regan staring at his shoes.

"Shoes are stuff that matters, coats, blankets, food. Computers, not so much."

She nodded.

"On our feet all day . . . gotta have good feet," Limpy muttered. His voice was low and he stuttered when he talked. When Regan looked at him, he turned his face away, pulled his hat over his eyes. He was short and thin, wearing a heavy, grey ski jacket, thick fleece pants, and heavy work boots.

"We been asking around about your mom and stuff," said Seb abruptly. "Not sure we learned much. But word is there's places they keep women, keep them working, trade them around. Not so good. Cops know about it but they don't know what to do. Too much money, too many guns."

"Some cops try," said Zack. "Some don't care."

"What was the name of that guy you went to see?" asked Seb.

"George . . . George Miller."

"Yeah, heard about him . . . he's a high roller, gambler,

probably drug dealer. Maybe got gang connections. Good thing you got the heck out of there, girlie."

Regan wrapped her arms around herself. She started to shake. Her mom might have been caught by a gang? What had she gotten into?

"Hey, you've scared her," Ramona said. "Honey, it don't mean anything. Seb is just talking. He doesn't really know anything. C'mon you guys, play a game, tell a story, something."

"Wait, someone's coming," Zack said. He stood up, drifted quietly into the darkness outside the ring of firelight.

"It might be Mike," Regan said.

"Yep, it's me," Mike said, stepping into the firelight. The light danced and tangled on the silver rings on his ears and in his eyebrows.

"Hey, dudes, look what I brought!" He began pulling chocolate bars out of jacket pockets.

"Some car drove into the window of that Seven-Eleven store downtown. Smashed the whole front off the place. Me, I headed for the chocolate."

He seemed happy, excited, dancing around the fire, throwing chocolate bars in people's laps. "And for you, beautiful ladies," he stopped and swept a low bow in front of Ramona and Regan, "a special treat!" And from under his coat, he pulled a whole bunch of long-stemmed red roses and handed half of them to Ramona and half to Regan.

Everyone began pulling wrappers off the chocolate bars

and, for a while, there was only the sound of satisfied munching around the fire.

"So who was driving the car?" Seb asked.

"Some guy had a heart attack or something."

"Old guy?"

"Dunno, no, younger, I think. I got in and out before the cops got there. People were all over the place, grabbing stuff. Lots of people helping too. Some people got him out of the car but I didn't stop to ask questions."

"Wow, thanks, Mike," Seb said. "We don't get chocolate around here every day. Rice and beans, stale bread. Not complainin', mind you, but I sure do love a little chocolate."

The talk turned to gossip about what was going on in the downtown neighbourhood, new buildings, and new people.

"Why don't they make a place we could carry shopping carts on the bus . . . you can take bikes on the sky train, why not shopping carts? Some days I swear I walk twenty miles in this city, up, down. Sure could use a break," said Zack.

"Keeps you healthy, gives you an appetite," said Rafe.

Mike had pulled his juggling balls out of his pockets and was idly flipping them back and forth.

"So, can you actually use those thing or you just got the fidgets?" Zack asked.

Mike grinned. He got to his feet, put the balls in his pocket, went to his backpack and pulled out three juggling pins, thin at the top, weighted at the bottom. He began to throw them up in the air, one, then two, then three, whizzing around in the firelight. Everyone applauded. He put down the pins, jumped on a log, began to juggle the balls, first two, then three, then four. When he was done, he did a backwards flip off the log and landed on his feet. Everyone applauded.

"Very cool, man," said Rafe, and everyone nodded.

"That was great," Zack said, "but we need to sleep. Mike, you got a sleeping bag?"

Mike nodded.

"Okay, well, you can bunk in with me. No snoring though."

Gradually, everyone drifted off to the tents. The fire had burned low. Ramona washed the teapot and dumped out the loose tea leaves on the fire.

Regan and Ramona crawled into Ramona's tent. They got into their sleeping bags and lay in the silence.

"You okay, baby?" Ramona asked. "I know something went wrong today. I could see it in your eyes. But you don't have to tell me unless you want to and it makes you feel better."

Regan sighed. "I saw that guy, George, today, in the coffee shop. Or he saw me. I ran and he came after me. Then I went to see if my grandma had sent me a bus ticket for Nicola Lake but it wasn't there."

"It's only been a couple of days."

"I know. I was afraid to come here tonight but I didn't know where else to go. What if they followed me here?"

"Takes a lot for anyone to find this place," Ramona said. "I put some safety spells over it. And Zack has a few tricks up his sleeve. He generally knows when someone is coming."

"You can do that? You can make spells?" Regan asked.

"When I don't have them wire noises in my head, I can do a lot of things. But if we have to leave here, then the noise gets in and I can't think."

"Why do you have to leave?"

"Too much rain. Can't keep warm, can't keep dry, can't get dry wood."

"Oh." She waited a bit. Then she asked, "Ramona, where do you think my mom went? Could you do a spell to find her?"

"I been thinking about that," Ramona said. "And I tried. She's somewhere, for sure. But every time I try to send my mind there, it feels kinda cold and dark. Not sure why. Maybe they got it wired, wherever she is."

Regan didn't really know what Ramona meant. She didn't really believe her but if Ramona thought her mom was alive, that was a tiny speck of comfort. Regan curled up in the darkness. The thin nylon floor under her was cold and her feet were freezing. She pulled part of the sleeping bag up over her head. She could tell from Ramona's heavy breathing that she was asleep. Thoughts and fears and pictures swirled around inside Regan's head. She had to make plans but she was so tired. Gradually she warmed up. She rubbed her icy feet against one another and furtively shoved them up against Ramona's broad, warm back. As her feet thawed, finally, she sank into the darkness.

Chapter Six

"GOT IT," MIKE SAID. He came down the alley where Regan was crouched behind a smelly dumpster.

"Wow, go Grandma," he said. He pulled the ticket out of the envelope, and two twenty-dollar bills fell out along with it. "Come on, let's move it. We can get a burger at the bus station."

Mike hustled her down the street towards the bus station, going ahead and checking each intersection for black vans. But they made it to the bus station with no incidents.

"It's a big city," Mike said as they came in the bus station door. "Hard to keep track of people. I think you're good to go, Regan McQueen, just get on the big dog, and get going.

Give me your email address. I can do some more checking on the George guy and his creepy friends. I'll use the computer at the library and send you what I find. You got that computer now so we can keep in touch. And I'll keep asking around. You know, no secrets on the street, babe, everybody talks."

She wrote down her email address for him, and then they looked at the bus schedule on the wall. They were in luck. A bus was leaving for Nicola Lake in an hour. They phoned Regan's grandmother who said she would be sure to meet the bus. Then Mike wanted to get hamburgers at the McDonald's inside the bus station, but Regan's stomach was clenched tight with nerves and fear and she couldn't eat. Mike finished her hamburger for her, grinned and said, "I'm going. Remember, check your email." And then he was gone.

It was a long three-hour bus ride over the mountains to Nicola Lake. Regan wondered if her grandmother had changed. It had been so long. What had she been, five or six, when they left? They had gone back periodically, and a few times, her mom had dropped her off and disappeared for a while. The last time this had happened, Regan was ten. She remembered lying in her room, listening to her grandmother and her mother argue. She couldn't hear the words, just the angry raised voices. In the morning, her mom had packed their car and they had left in a hurry.

Her grandmother had kept in touch, had sent Christmas and birthday presents, birthday cards, and even the occasional postcard. But Regan's mom never talked about her. Her mom always made her write thank-you cards for the gifts and they always picked out a birthday card for her grandmother's birthday. But that was it.

As the bus pulled into the shopping centre on the edge of town, Regan spotted her grandmother immediately, standing right on the edge of the sidewalk. She was peering anxiously at the bus as it pulled up to the sidewalk. Regan was first off the bus and ran to her grandmother, who threw her arms around Regan and held on as if she were drowning.

"Oh, my goodness, I have missed you more than I could ever say. Oh Regan, you are so big, and tall, and beautiful! Oh my, oh my." And she wrapped her arms around Regan again. Except the strange thing was, her head only came to Regan's shoulder. Regan had always thought of her grandmother as big and strong. Now she realized her grandmother's hair was grey, her face was wrinkled, and her shoulders sagged under her worn blue raincoat. Her grandmother led the way to a small white car, and they drove out of town down the winding highway that to Regan was both familiar and strange. She stared out the window, trying to see everything.

The house, when they reached it, was like a picture slowly coming into focus. As Regan got out of the car, grabbed her backpack and came up the brick walk to the screen door, it was like scrolling backwards in a familiar movie. Yes, there was the lawn where she had once ridden her tricycle, there was the lake, just below the house where she used to throw rocks into the water. And as she came into the house, what hit her most was the familiar smell, a smell that was oddly comforting, the smell of baking and flowers and floor polish and home.

Regan automatically took her backpack down the hall to her old room. It looked just the same, the narrow bed with a patchwork quilt, the white lace curtains, the painting on the wall. She sank onto the bed, her face in her hands.

"I kept it for you," her grandmother said softly, from the doorway. "I always knew you would come back."

"I remember it so clearly," Regan said. "It seems like yesterday I was here."

"Well, you lived here for a whole year when you were six. When you left, you had just started grade two."

Regan stared. "I don't remember that. I stayed that long?"

"Come and have a snack, sweetie. I made cookies, and there's lemonade, or juice. What would you like?"

Regan followed her grandmother out to the kitchen, sat at the old wooden table and looked out the window through the yellow checked curtains. It was all so familiar. She felt as if she had been here just a few days ago but she also felt as if she had stepped back in time—as if she were a different person from the one she had been just a day ago.

Her grandmother was smiling at her. "You sure do look like your daddy," she said. "You even talk and walk like him."

"I do?"

"Do you remember him?"

"Not really."

"Well, if you feel like it, we'll get out the old photo albums after dinner, have a look. Are you hungry?"

Regan nodded. She was hungry, she realized. Starving, in fact. As if she hadn't eaten for days, even though, aside from a bite of the hamburger at the station, it had been only this morning that she had eaten a lovely bagel toasted over the fire at the camp in the brush. Ramona had hugged her for a long time when she left.

"You take care," Ramona had called after her. "Just be very, very careful."

Her grandma cooked hamburgers, with slices of cheese, cucumber and tomato. There was apple juice to drink, and homemade lemon cake for dessert. Regan ate two loaded hamburgers, gulped down three glasses of juice and then stuffed down two pieces of lemon cake. After supper, they piled the dishes in the sink and then Grandma brought out two big photo albums filled with pictures of Regan's mom, dad, and herself as a child. The album was thick and they examined every page.

Regan began to yawn. She hadn't slept much in the past week.

Her grandmother smiled. "Time for bed."

Regan slept long and deeply. When she woke in the morning, sun shone in on the yellow walls of her room. There was a child's drawing on the wall, a picture of Regan's mother. She had drawn it in grade one and her grandmother had had it framed. Now it was hanging on the wall. And there, on the bureau, was a picture of her mom and dad.

She got up and went to the bureau and picked up the photo. Her mom and dad were standing together in a garden, smiling and laughing. Both of them were looking at the camera. Her dad was tall, broad shouldered, handsome. A wave of longing swept over Regan. If only she had known him. She hugged the picture to her chest. Her throat hurt. If only her dad were still here.

She looked at it again, at her mom, young and beautiful, sunlight on her hair. "Mom, come home, please," she whispered.

She heard her grandmother calling her for breakfast. Reluctantly, she put the picture back down. Maybe her grandmother could make her a copy.

She could smell bacon cooking. Her grandma was standing at the kitchen stove, while the radio spun a patter of noise.

There was a plate of hot biscuits with butter and honey, bacon and eggs, and a jug of orange juice on the table. Regan sat down and loaded up her plate. When she was done, Regan sighed and said, "Grandma, that was the best breakfast I ever ate."

"You always did like my biscuits," her grandma said. "Now, what should we do today? I'm afraid I can't walk very far, but we can always drive somewhere."

"Why can't you walk?"

"Oh, my heart has been acting up, nothing serious, Regan.

Don't worry about me. I get along just fine. I've got good neighbours who keep an eye out for me."

But Regan noticed her grandma's hands, bent and gnarled, and how she walked slowly when she went to put the dishes in the sink. Occasionally, she would pause and lean on a chair.

"Grandma?"

"Yes?"

"What did you and my mom fight about, that last time we were here?"

"I wanted her to leave you here with me while she went to look for work. I thought she should go find a job and a place to live first, and I told her I didn't think the city was a good place for you. You liked to be outside. You were so happy here. And I was being selfish. I didn't want to lose you. But there was other stuff too." Grandma sighed. "Your mom and I didn't agree on a lot of things. I was too hard on her. She was so torn up by your dad dying. All she wanted to do was go out and party and have fun and try and forget. I thought she should stay home and look after you. I was too hard on her. I realize that now."

"She's a good mom."

"I know, honey. You and your mom really love each other. But I worry about where you're living, downtown like you are. There's so much bad news about that area these days."

"It's okay."

"But aren't there a lot of drugs and homeless people?"

"I'm pretty careful. I study kung fu," said Regan. "Sifu says drugs are poison and I agree with him. And most of the home-less people are okay. Some of them are really nice."

"Okay, if you say so. But I sure wish you lived in a better part of town."

"Mom doesn't have a car so we live where she can walk to work and I can walk to school."

"Oh, I see. So where did your mom go this time?"

"She's working as a hostess at a big party."

"A card party?"

"I don't know."

"Your mom sure loves to play cards, poker mostly."

"No, she doesn't! She doesn't play cards at all."

Grandma looked at Regan. "Well, maybe you're right. She used to like to play cards, she and your dad. But that was a long time ago."

There was silence in the kitchen. "Come on," said her grand-ma. "I think I can walk as far as the beach. Remember how you used to love making sand castles?"

"Grandma! That was when I was little."

"Well, I'm sure we can find something to do at the beach. Put on your coat. This time in September there can be a cold wind."

They spent the morning at the beach. They went for a long slow walk and sat in the sun. Then after a lunch of grilled cheese sandwiches and chicken soup, they played Scrabble until it was time for Regan's grandmother to have a nap. Regan played on her computer until she got sleepy and then she had a nap too. Her grandma made dinner, fried chicken and mashed potatoes. Regan thought she had never eaten so much good food in her life. And just as they finished cleaning up and doing the dishes, they both heard a car door slam.

"That's odd," grandma said. "Who would be coming here at this time of night?"

Regan jumped from her chair and ran to the kitchen window that looked out to the driveway. It was the black van and two men were getting out of it.

"Grandma," she hissed. "I'm not here, you never saw me." Panicked, she ran down the hall to her room. She could hear her grandma calling, "What? Regan, what's going on? Come back here."

Instead, she closed the bedroom door and then stared around. This was stupid. This wasn't a refuge. The men would find her here in a second. Where could she go? Where was the back door to this house? Oh, right, it was in the basement. There was a sliding glass door on the living room that led out to the deck but she would have to go through the kitchen to get there.

She slipped out of her room, ran back down the hall to the basement stairs and went down them two steps at a time. In the dark basement, she stopped. She heard the men knock on the door, heard her grandmother go to answer it, heard their muffled voices and then their footsteps as they came inside the kitchen. What could she do? What if they hurt her grandmother?

She began to tiptoe carefully back up the basement stairs. She needed to hear what was happening.

"She's not here," her grandmother said. "I haven't seen Joanie or Regan for years. They never come here."

"Listen, old lady," said a man's voice. "You'd better be straight with us or else. We need to find your daughter-in-law and we need to find her fast. And if her kid knows where she is, then we're going to find her too and make her talk."

"You get out of here," Grandma said. "The nerve of you, young man, coming here at night and threatening an old lady. Just who do you think you are? Get out of my house, right now."

"We're not going until we get some answers that make sense. We been looking for this chick for three weeks. No trace of her. Somebody knows something. And we figure that kid came here. We was watching the apartment. We saw her get on the bus so we followed along. We asked around town for a Joanie Anderson and they said she used to live here. So if she ain't here, where else would she go?"

"I haven't the faintest idea." Grandma's voice was shaky. "You get out of my house, you stupid man."

No way could Regan leave her grandmother alone to deal with this. She stomped into the kitchen.

"You leave my grandma alone," she said. Her voice shook. She couldn't control it.

"Regan, what is going on? Who are these men?" her grandma asked.

Her grandma's face was so white, Regan worried she might faint. Her grandma was leaning on the back of a chair.

"Okay, kid, just tell us where your mom is and we'll get out of here and leave you alone." It was the bigger of the two men speaking. He was tall, but his bulging belly spilled over his belt buckle. His head was bald and he had two crosses tattooed on his face. Regan's heart froze. Mike had told her those tattoos meant someone had been in jail.

The other man was shorter, red-headed, with tiny mean eyes. He had crosses tattooed on every knuckle.

"We been chasing your mother for three weeks. She's got some money that don't belong to her."

"I haven't seen her. I don't know where she is."

"You met George, girlie. He ain't a nice guy and he ain't fooling around. He sent us to find you. George is nasty when he's upset."

Regan felt a sudden rush of fury. "My mom isn't a thief. She didn't take your stupid money. She would never do that. And you scared my grandma. She's got a bad heart."

"Regan, call the police," her grandma said. "Right now."

"Nope, you don't want to do that," the tall man said. "Just answer our questions and we'll be gone. We're talking a lot of money here. If your mom didn't take it, then she sure knows who did. We find her, we find the money. Simple."

"How much money."

"Couple of million, more or less."

Regan gulped in a breath, and felt herself grow dizzy. She

shook her head. "Well, my mom didn't take it. Maybe she knows who did, and that person kidnapped her."

"Yeah, we thought of that, too," said the big man. "But no one's seen her. Or so they say."

Regan stared at them. "I haven't seen my mom. She went away. I'm living on my own." There was another thought about her mother that Regan kept pushing away. She slammed into a chair and put her head in her hands.

The room went very silent.

"Okay," Grandma said calmly, "here's what you're going to do. You're going to leave here now. Obviously, we don't know anything."

Regan lifted her head stared at her. How could her grandma be so calm? The two men stared at her as well.

"We don't know anything about any money. Regan is living here now with me. And Regan is right. Her mother would never steal anything. So please, just go."

Suddenly Regan's grandmother leaned over and closed her eyes. She put one hand on her chest.

"Grandma!" said Regan.

"I have to sit down," she whispered. "Need my pills. In the bathroom. By the sink."

Regan helped her into a chair, ran to the bathroom. There were several bottles of pills. She grabbed them all and ran back. The men were both on their feet, looking confused, as if they couldn't decide what to do.

"That one," whispered Grandma. "Get it open, get me some water."

Regan charged to the sink, grabbed a glass, filled it with water, ran back, knelt beside her grandmother, and held the glass so she could drink.

"Help me to the bedroom," Regan's grandmother whispered. "I have to lie down."

"I'll call an ambulance," Regan said.

"No, the medication will work. It just needs time."

Regan held her arm, helped her into the bedroom. She lay down and Regan covered her with a quilt. Her grandmother lay back and closed her eyes. "I just have to lie quiet for a bit until the pill kicks in," she said. "Then I'll be okay. Don't worry about me, Regan, my love. I've dealt with this before. Don't go back out there with those horrible men. Stay here with me."

Regan sat on the bed until her grandmother's breathing seemed to indicate that she was asleep. Then she went back out to the kitchen.

The two men were still sitting there.

"What's going on?" asked the redhead. "Lenny, go have a look. If that old lady croaks, George will skin us."

Lenny stood up, went to the bedroom. Regan jumped to her feet. "You leave her alone," she yelled.

Lenny stomped back into the kitchen. "Aw, she's all right," he said. "Looks like she's sleeping."

"No, she's not," Regan said. "Thanks to you. And she's got one of those emergency bracelets. It calls the ambulance automatically. They'll be here right away."

The redhead sighed. "Look kid, we'll get out of here for

now, but we ain't done with you, you little brat. If we find out you lied to us, we'll be back, and next time, Grandma will have more than a little heart trouble, if you get my drift."

The bigger man said, "The sooner you find your mother, the better for everyone. All she's gotta do is tell us who took the money and we'll leave you all alone. I figure you're looking for her too, just like us. So if you do know where your mom is, or you find out, all you gotta do is tell her to hand over the money or tell us who took it. Got it?"

The big man looked at the redhead. Some signal passed between them.

"Okay, we're out of here for now," the redhead said. They both turned, headed for the back door, and were gone.

Regan sat down at the table. She held onto it with both hands.

"Are they gone?" her grandma asked from the bedroom door.

"Grandma, are you okay?"

"Yes, I'll live." Regan's grandma's voice was still very shaky. "No, don't get up. Just sit. I am going to make tea with a lot of sugar, because we're both in shock. We're going to drink it and you are going to tell me everything that is going on." But her grandma's hands were shaking so hard as she went to fill the kettle at the sink that she had to rest it against the tap where it rattled and clanked until she got it back onto the counter and plugged it in.

While her grandmother made the tea, Regan kept staring at the black window.

What was she going to do now? She had run out of safe places, she had endangered her grandmother, and she still had no idea where her mother had gone. The two men had terrified her. What would they do to her mother if they found her? All of these thoughts whirled around her head as her grandmother set mugs of sweetened hot milky tea on the table.

"Drink it," Regan's grandma said. "It will help."

Regan really didn't want the tea but she took a big gulp and then another. It did seem to help. The heat and the sugar went down inside and melted the frozen lump of fear and panic in her stomach.

"Better?" her grandma asked. Regan nodded.

"Now," her grandma said. "Where is your mother? Why are you here? And who were those horrible men?"

Regan sighed, then took a big breath. Once she began to talk, she felt a huge relief at being able to tell someone the whole story. She told her grandmother about her mom going off with the strange man, of her growing fear as the food and money disappeared, of going to school every day with a knot in her stomach, of her habit of sitting on the roof of the abandoned house and watching the street, evening after evening. And then about Mike, about going to the hotel, finding George's address, and going to the blue apartment building. About her terror at George grabbing her arm and fleeing. About finding the break-in at the apartment, going to the group home and running away, and then seeing George in the coffee shop, running away from the men in the black van, and getting on the bus. She left out the part about the camp under the bridge.

It took a while to tell it all. Her grandmother was silent, except for a couple of questions when she wasn't clear about Regan's story. When it was over she sat back.

"Regan," she said. "I love your mom and I know she loves you, more than anything. Yes, we had a fight, a stupid fight. But I know your mom would never leave you alone for a long time if she could help it. You're right, she's in terrible trouble. And we need to figure out how to help her. What about the police?"

"I talked to them. They seemed to think my mom was a bad mom. They didn't say it but I could tell that was what they thought. They don't even know her! They wouldn't look for her. They just stuck me in a group home and left."

"Well, you have to call them again now. You have to make them listen."

"But where could my mom be?"

"I have no idea."

Regan's grandma leaned over and took her hand.

"Oh my sweet baby," she said. "My beautiful Regan."

They sat like that for a long, long time, too exhausted to move, and too frightened to go to sleep.

Chapter Seven

THE SQUAT WAS VERY quiet in the morning. Most people were sleeping off the excesses of the night before. From her mattress in the attic, Regan could hear rain on the roof, a gull squawking, distant traffic that sounded more like wind than cars, and Mike snoring on the mattress on the other side of the room. She couldn't hear much of what went on in the rest of the house.

Regan sat up. She kept her sleeping bag wrapped around her shoulders. It was cold in the old house. During the day, if someone had managed to scrounge enough firewood somewhere, there might be a fire in the fireplace downstairs. But the residents of the squat rarely lit the fireplace during the day in case someone came and asked about the smoke. There was a propane stove in the kitchen. If someone had some money, they could get propane at a gas station several blocks away. But there was never enough propane to use for heat. Regan was mostly just very, very cold. And hungry.

She had stayed with her grandmother for a week, but by then she knew she had to leave. Her grandmother had, at first, refused to let her return to the city. They argued. Her grandmother cried.

"I have to find my mom," Regan said.

"But it's not safe. There's no one to look after you. Just let the police look for your mom. It's their job. I want you here with me. I need to know that you're safe."

"I've got friends to stay with."

"What friends?"

"I can stay with my teacher, Mary Harris. Or with my friend, Mike."

Regan had finally burst into tears, promised she would stay with her teacher, promised she would be okay, that she wouldn't take chances.

So, by lying her face off, she had persuaded her grandmother to let her come back to the city. She said that she would stay in contact with the police, and that everything would be fine.

Regan could see her grandmother didn't believe her, but finally she was just too tired to argue any more.

And when Regan got down off the bus, she had gone to the

camp under the bridge only to find that it had been abandoned.

In the rain, it had been desolate. The leaves were almost all off the trees and brush. All that remained of the campfire was a burnt circle on the ground. The planks for the table were gone. The chairs were gone. The logs that people had sat on were gone. The only other sign her friends had been there was the flattened grass in the places where there had been a circle of brightly coloured tents.

That night she slept in the abandoned camp, making a kind of cold bed of leaves under the brush. The next day she went looking. She had found Ramona on the street downtown, standing in the waiting line for lunch outside the church, but Ramona hadn't appeared to recognize her. She was with Annie. Ramona was mumbling to herself and bobbing her head. Annie appeared to be taking care of her. They both had shopping carts full of stuff; they were sharing a cigarette.

She had seen Zack as well but he was too drunk to know who she was.

So she had found Mike, and he had taken her to an abandoned house where he and a few other street people appeared to be living, at least temporarily. It was always hard to tell with Mike. She told him about her grandmother, about the men, and he just listened and didn't say much.

Then he sighed. "Reggie, I been asking around, you know. A couple of people I talked to figure your mom might have gone south with this guy, this Dimitri. There's some stories on the street about what happened. People are talking, saying your mom stole money, ran off with some Russian dude."

"No, she didn't. I know she didn't. She wouldn't do that."

"Yeah, it's all just gossip. Regan, you gotta talk to the cops again."

But she refused. And then one night, while she was lying curled up in her damp sleeping bag, Mike said, unexpectedly, into the darkness, "You know, Regan, maybe going to the group home wouldn't be so bad. You could go back to school, maybe get some new clothes. You gotta start thinking about what comes next."

She sat up in bed. "What do you mean, what comes next?"

"Well, you know, if your mom doesn't come home. If something has happened to her."

"My mom's not dead. Ramona told me she was somewhere. Ramona could sense it. I'm going to find her. She's coming home."

"Oh, Regan," Mike said, and sighed. "Yeah, well, whatever you say."

Regan curled up again. She pulled the sleeping bag over her head but it didn't help. Jolts of adrenaline shot through her muscles. Her heart pounded furiously. It wasn't true. Her mom was coming back. She had to believe that or she had no future at all. But at the same time, she couldn't help understanding what Mike had just said. If her mom didn't come back, Regan was going to have to do something with her life. On her own.

She could go back to her grandmother's. Her grandmother would take her in. In fact, her grandma had suggested it, over and over. But Regan had seen her after those men had finally left. Had seen her shaking hands, her white face. Her grandmother had gone to bed early that night, and the next day she spent most of the day in an armchair, covered in an afghan, alternately dozing and waking and then dozing off again. Regan had made her tea and soup, had done the dishes and made the beds.

But by the second day, her grandmother was up and trying to work around the house. Regan helped as much as she could but her grandmother kept saying, "I'm fine, don't you worry about me."

In fact, Regan thought her grandmother had been secretly relieved to see her go, though she knew her grandmother would never say such a thing.

Or she could meekly go back to the group home, live in a tiny room with a narrow bed, a desk, a table lamp and ugly curtains. Get up, go to school, eat the crappy food, say yes and no and study and read, and maybe someday have a life. And never know where her mother went, or if she had suffered, or if she had wondered and worried about Regan, if she was even dead or alive.

Regan tossed and turned. A streetlight shone in the uncurtained cracked window. It was too cold to get up, and yet she was too restless, too worried, too wired on fear and sadness to lie there any longer. Finally she did get up. Mike didn't move—she could hear his breath whistling through his nose—she could even see his breath, and hers. Quickly she slipped on her coat—she had worn her clothes to bed—slid her backpack with the laptop on her back, pulled on her wet runners, and tiptoed down the creaky stairs. She had no idea what time it was. There was no clock in the squat, although several of the people who came and went had cellphones and Regan had the laptop. She never brought the computer out when other people were around, however. She was too afraid she would wake one morning and it would be gone.

She had no idea where she was going, either. She just knew she couldn't lie still. She had to move, had to keep moving, to keep the feelings in her stomach, which felt like red-hot stones, from settling there and burning a hole in her belly. She decided she would wander past her old apartment building and at least check the mail. She still had the mail key in her pocket. Hopefully the landlord hadn't changed it. Regan and her mom had never received anything but bills, but it was something to do.

It wasn't that late. There were still people on the street, lots of cars. Of course, the downtown city never really went to bed. About the time the partiers and the people who had been drinking themselves stupid went home, the early morning people—cooks, bakers, cleaners, people who opened doors and set out signs—were already on their way to work.

Regan trotted quietly along until she got to the familiar building. She stopped, checked the street. Maybe someone was still watching it. But the street was quiet. All the parked cars looked empty. Finally she crossed to the door. It was supposed to be locked but in reality it never was.

Regan slid the key in the mailbox slot, twisted it. There was a stack of mail, a phone bill, an electric bill, a gas bill, fliers for Chinese restaurants, Greek restaurants, Thai restaurants. And one small plain white sealed envelope with no address. She turned it over and over. There were no clues. Finally, she tore it open. She thought it was empty at first, and then when she looked more closely, she saw there was a tiny sticker in there, the kind of sticker a teacher might put in a schoolbook for little kids, a crown sticker, with flowers on it. But she had seen that sticker before. Her mom had bought a sheet of them for a joke, the night before she left. She and Regan had been buying milk at a corner store. The stickers were hanging beside the cash register and her mom had paid for them and slid them into her purse.

Regan slid down the wall until she was sitting on the floor. She stared at the sticker, thinking, and then she ran out of the building, down the alley, and dodged across the streets until she got to the squat. She went in through the broken back door, felt her way carefully through the dim grey light to the stairs and then went up three flights to the attic. Mike was still asleep. Regan sat on the floor beside him.

"Mike, wake up!"

He woke up instantly, rolled over, came up with a knife in one hand.

"Mike, it's Regan, calm down."

His eyes focused on her, and he took a deep breath. "Regan, don't ever wake me up like that again, okay."

"Yeah, sorry, sorry, Mike, but I have to tell you something. It's my mom, she's alive, she's in the city. She sent me a message, well, a kind of message."

He sat up. "Regan, it's too cold for this. Here, you're shaking, come crawl in with me and get warm." He moved over on the mattress and she slid off her wet coat and crawled in beside him. She was shaking, both from excitement and cold, and Mike was warm beside her. She told him about getting up, about checking the postbox, and finding the sticker. But she kept shaking. She couldn't calm down.

"Mike, I've got to find her," she said. "I've just got to. What can I do, where can I go now?"

Mike sighed. "Yeah, yeah, it's great. But you can't do anything in the middle of the night. The best thing you can do is get some sleep. In the morning, we'll go find some food, and then we'll make a plan."

"I can't sleep."

"Well, I can and I'm going to."

It felt weird lying beside Mike. They were just friends. She had never thought of him as anything more. There was so much she didn't know about him and his life, like the parties he went to. She didn't know if she could really trust him.

"Regan," he said drowsily. "We're just staying warm. I'm your friend, baby. Now let's get some sleep."

Soon, she could hear from his deep, even breathing that he had fallen asleep. And so, eventually, did she, as the warmth from Mike and her own exhaustion coaxed her finally into sleep.

She woke early, still elated from her discovery. She got up, feeling grubby from wearing the same clothes she had worn the day before and the day before that.

She had come home from her grandmother's three days ago with a suitcase of new clean clothes, packages of sandwiches and cookies, and a hundred dollars tucked into the lining of her backpack. She kept the backpack with her all the time, even though it was heavy.

Mike had warned her the first night. "Don't trust anyone in the squat. Even if they seem nice. They're not. They'll steal anything you have." She took him at his word. She hadn't told him about the money or the food either. She felt bad about it but she didn't know who to trust. Why was Mike hanging out in this freezing house? Why didn't he have a family, somewhere to go? He had never talked to her about his personal life, except when he disappeared to what he vaguely called, "a party."

She took one of the last of the cheese sandwiches out of her backpack, unwrapped it and ate it in small bites. She was so hungry she could have eaten several more sandwiches. She had one left—and a few packages of cookies, some juice boxes. She drank one of the juice boxes. She'd save the rest for later.

Now, what to do? She needed information. She needed to

talk to that woman cop, and most of all, she needed to find out about Clayton, the man she and Mike had first encountered in the hotel. He had given them George's address. She realized now he had set her up by sending her to George. He had wanted George to kidnap her so they could question her about her mother. Was he still in the city? She pulled the laptop out of her backpack, wrapped her sleeping bag around her shoulders, and turned it on. There was a faint WiFi connection in the house from a nearby coffee shop, not much, but enough. She began to search. After half an hour, she had a lot more information on poker and poker games than she had ever wanted to know, but no real information. She searched for phone numbers and addresses for the two men she knew were involved; George's address she knew but she wondered if something more might come up.

And then, sure enough, after she had clicked through page after page of links, she found a story in a magazine about a high stakes poker game that had both men's names in it. So at least she could be sure they knew each other. The police had to check this out. They could find Clayton and this Dimitri guy and get the truth out of them. Wasn't there some kind of international police force that could just go to Vegas or wherever he lived and pick him up?

Mike groaned, rolled over and sat up. "God," he said. "I need coffee. You got any money, Regan?"

"A little bit," she said cautiously.

"Yeah, I expected your grandma would give you something.

Don't worry, all I need is a coffee. But if you got any money, keep it hidden."

"Right."

"By the way, I'm sorry about last night," Mike added.

"Sorry about what?"

"I didn't want you to think I was coming on to you or anything. I would never do that. It's just, well, you were so cold and shaky." She looked at him. His face was red.

"It's okay," she said. "It was so nice to be warm. It put me to sleep."

"Regan, I'd never hurt you, I want you to know that."

"Okay," she said again, but puzzled. "You're my friend, pretty much the only one I have right now."

"Well, that's a start," he said.

She looked at him, puzzled. "A start to what?"

"Oh, never mind. I'm not too good at this friendship stuff. I never really had many friends."

"But you know lots of people, all over the city."

"Knowing people and being their friend isn't the same thing."

"I guess not."

There was silence in the chilly bare attic. Regan wanted to ask him more questions about his life but she didn't want him to think she was prying into things. Into his past. Into what he did when he disappeared for long periods.

"C'mon, let's go," he said. "We'll get a coffee, we'll get warm. And you can tell me why you're so sure your mom is somewhere around the city."

On the way to the coffee shop around the corner, she told him about the sticker, pulled it out of her backpack, stroked it gently and put it back in the envelope. The sun was shining on the piles of soggy brown leaves lining gutters beside the sidewalks. The sun lit up her face and hair and warmed the deep chill in her bones. She felt a sudden completely unreasonable surge of happiness.

When they were seated in the coffee shop, she ordered breakfast for both of them. Even though she had just eaten the sandwich, she was still starving. Mike just watched her, an amused smile on his face, and didn't say anything until the food came.

They both ate without speaking, gulping down the food, and washing it down with coffee and then coffee refills. Regan felt the coffee hit her body with a jolt. She was suddenly dizzy; her heart was racing but it eventually passed and she shook her head to clear it. She never used to like coffee and now she couldn't live without it.

When they were done, Mike leaned back. "So what are we doing to do?"

Regan noted that "we." Until now, Mike had seemed to feel that her vanished mother was her problem. He might feel sorry for her, but that was it. In fact, she had begun to wonder if she was crazy or if everyone else was. Other people seemed to think that her mother was a jerk, and Regan was somehow better off without her—that all she had to do was forget about her mother and get on with her own life. Even her grandmother seemed to think that Regan's mother went to too many parties and card games. No way was she going to let go of caring for her mother and searching for her. She would never do that.

Over their last coffee refill, she told Mike about her internet search.

"Well, I could probably find that Clay dude again, I guess," he said. "I heard on the street he was back in town. I don't know how much he would tell me though. I never asked him about what he does before. And, Regan, you really need to talk to the cops again. You have to persuade them to take this thing seriously."

"And how do I do that without getting thrown in a group home again?"

"Here's a phone," he said, pulling an old cell phone out of his pocket. "There's still some time on it. If you run out, you just need to buy some more minutes for it. They can't trace you."

"Okay. What we do," Regan said, "is find where this Clayton guy is. And then we watch him. That's what those two creeps in the black van were going to do."

"And how do you suggest we do that?"

"I don't know. We need a car."

"Yeah, right, we're street kids, living in a freezing filthy squat. You got a car in that backpack somewhere?"

She looked at him.

"Sorry," Mike said. "Sometimes I just really, really hate my life."

"You do?"

"Oh, forget it," he said. "This is about you, not me."

"But it is about you too. You're helping me. You're involved."

"Yeah, don't remind me." He put his head in his hands and shook his head back and forth. "Sorry, I'm not good at involvement. I'm good at staying uninvolved. Been practising it for a long time." He stood up. "I'm going to the park, do my juggling for the people. On such a nice day, there should be some pennies in it. Come and find me there."

Regan watched him go. She picked up the phone. She had that card the cop had given her tucked away in her backpack. She fished it out—punched in the cop's number.

"Brenda Silsbie here, how can I help you?"

"Hi Brenda, this is Regan Anderson, remember, my mom went missing and you said you would look for her."

There was a long pause. "Oh, yeah, right, and you were supposed to stay in a group home and be safe. Where are you now, Regan?"

"I'm fine, I'm safe, I have people to stay with."

"Is that so? Why don't I believe you? Sounds like you're in a coffee shop right now. Why don't we meet up? We can talk about anything you want."

"My mom is alive," Regan said. "Why aren't you looking for her?" Her voice sounded shrill, even to her.

"Who says we're not? Regan, if you have any new information, I'd be happy to hear it."

So Regan told her, in a rush, about the trip to her grandmother's, about the men and what they looked like, about the Russian guy, Dimitri, the poker games, the crown sticker in the mail box, George, Clayton, black vans. It didn't come out very clearly and even to her, it sounded confusing.

At the other end, Brenda finally said, "Whoa, whoa, I write fast but I can't keep track of who or what or where. Look, Regan, let me come and meet you. If you say you're okay for now, I'll take you at your word. Do you know Sarah? The youth worker down there? I can bring her with me if you want. This is just too confusing over the phone. Regan, I'd really like to help you out, but you're sure not making it easy."

"Just check out this Clayton guy." And just as she said that, the phone went dead.

"Oh crap," she said. The waitress had been looking at her for a while. The coffee shop was crowded and Regan was sitting at a table with four chairs, in front of an empty coffee cup. Time to move. She paid for their breakfast and, as Regan left the coffee shop, she checked the time on the clock on the wall. The clock had a calendar beside it. Tuesday. Oh no, it was her kung fu day. She had missed last week. What would Sifu be thinking after he had offered her free lessons and a chance to be in a tournament? Maybe she should go by the studio, see if he was there, talk to him.

Outside, the sun was bright and almost warm. People hurried by, intent on their lives. The street outside the coffee shop was crowded with cars, buses, and trucks. Regan hesitated.

A man sitting on the sidewalk outside the coffee shop, face

turned up to the sun, a yellow dog lying beside him, said, "Hey, cutie, got some time for me?" She shook her head. The man had long tangled hair, and was missing teeth. He reminded her a little bit of Zack. She wondered, briefly, where Ramona and Zack and the others had gone.

The light changed and the traffic began to move. Regan stepped briskly down the sidewalk, her backpack shifting softly back and forth against her shoulders. One of her friends at school had told her that one way of staying safe in the downtown area was to walk fast and always to look as if she were going somewhere, as if she were a busy person, with things to do and places to go. Otherwise, the street would sense her hesitation, she would become visible to predators and other street people.

She cut through stinking alleyways, past dumpsters and back doors, until she got to the studio where Sifu taught classes. It was early still; he might not be there yet. She stood in front of the door, hesitating, then knocked.

Sifu opened the door. "Regan," he said. "Come in. I missed you last you week. You are one of my best students. When you stay away, I worry."

She followed him into a small office. "Sit down," he said. "Where is your mother? Have you heard anything? Sarah came to see me. Police talk to her. She talk to me. Everyone worries about you." He stared at her, frowned. He had very black, very kind eyes.

"She's somewhere in the city," Regan said. "She left me a sticker, in the mailbox." She fished it out and showed it to him. He turned it over and around, looked at it closely, handed it back.

"Where are you staying?"

There was no point in lying to Sifu. "In a squat," she said. "It's pretty horrible. Cold, but okay, I guess."

Sifu leaned back, put his hands behind his head.

"You stay here," he said. "Here is office, kitchen, small bed in back room. Not being used at night. No one will find you. Alarm system. Stay here."

"Really?"

"Yes, really. Regan, you are a very fine person and your mom is a good mom. She works hard. She tries hard. You can use the phone and computer, find your mother."

Regan opened her mouth, closed it again. She was going to ask about Mike but she stopped.

"What is it?" Sifu asked.

"I have a friend, well, a sort of friend, Mike, he's a juggler, he's been helping me."

"No," Sifu said. "Only you. I know Mike. I see him juggling, but I don't really know him well. You, I trust."

Regan sighed. Why did every good thing in her life come with such sharp edges? Mike was just beginning to open up to her. If she left him now, he might think she didn't want to see him anymore. Well, she would decide later. Right now, she had to call Brenda again.

"I am going to teach," Sifu said. "Stay here, food in the kitchen, rest." He went out to his class.

But she couldn't rest and she couldn't relax. She dialed

Brenda's number again. "I am out of the office for now. Please leave a number and I will call you back."

"Brenda, this is Regan, can you call me at this number?" She left Sifu's number. She could hear his class outside the door, the deep shouts, squeaks of their shoes on the floor, thud of bodies on mats. She pulled the laptop out of her backpack and plugged it in, but there was no more information and she couldn't think of places to look. She checked a few websites anyway.

"Regan," said a voice from the door. She looked up, startled. It was Brenda.

"Relax," Brenda said. She sat down in the chair beside the desk. "I knew the number so I knew where you were. I just talked to Sifu. The thing is, he's my teacher too and I trust him. He told me quite a few things about you, that you're a good person and so is your mom. He says you're staying here and you're safe for now, so I am going to let that stand. For now. But it's a temporary solution, Regan. If we can't find your mom, or if she doesn't come back, you are going to have to go into a group home, or a foster home. Somewhere safe where you can be looked after, and where you can get your butt back in school. Your teacher tells me you are, or at least you used to be, a good student. Don't mess that up."

"I can go to my grandma's house if I have to," Regan said. "But it doesn't matter because my mom is coming back."

"Regan, I checked out this Clayton. I talked to him at his hotel. I'm sorry, Regan. He denies any knowledge of your mom and he was alone at the hotel. He says he remembers her from the poker game but he hasn't seen her since. I don't know if there is anything more I can do."

Regan stared at Brenda. Her heart turned into a tiny frozen stone. She could feel it happening. She pulled the sticker in its envelope out of her jacket pocket. "Then what about this?"

Brenda took it, looked at it, turned it over. "Hmm, this was in the mailbox, right?"

"Yes."

"Regan, I am going to take this in for forensic analysis. I doubt if it will tell us anything but we'll give it a try." She stood up again. "Regan," she said, "I'm so sorry, but crappy stuff happens down here all the time. People go missing. Women go missing. It's not a safe place. You need to decide what you're going to do. My advice to you is to go back to your grandmother's and let us handle this. We'll buy you a bus ticket if that is what you want." Brenda hesitated. "Regan, I owe you an apology. Sifu tells me I misjudged you and your mom. Okay, I'll do what I can and I'll be in touch."

She marched briskly out of the room. Regan stared after her. And then she pulled her knees up to her chest, put her head on her knees, closed her eyes, and let the pain from what Brenda had just said wash over her like frozen fire.

Much later back at the squat, Regan told Mike about the conversation with Brenda. "She was nice but she didn't seem to think there was much she could do. There has to be something they can do to find my mom."

"Maybe they'll put up a missing persons poster or something. But she's right, Regan. People go missing all the time. The cops don't do much about it."

"You should have heard her. It was like she was telling me to just forget about my mom."

"I don't think she would say that. She's a cop. They always pretend to be nice."

"But that's what she really meant, underneath. I could tell."

Mike and Regan were lying side by side in the attic of the squat. They had put Regan's sleeping bag underneath them and Mike's on top and they were both warm. They lay close together, just barely touching. Regan had told Mike about Sifu's offer, but she hadn't told Mike the offer was just for her and not for him. She had thought it over. She didn't want to be alone, and besides, she couldn't leave Mike in that horribly lonely squat by himself. So after she had left the studio, she pocketed the keys Sifu had given her and set off to find Mike.

"I'm stuck," Regan said. "I'm really stuck, aren't I? I might never know what happened. I might never find her. No matter what I do. No matter how hard I try."

"Regan, don't give up."

"I'll never give up."

He reached over, took her hand, squeezed it and let go again.

They lay side by side in the dark, breathing. Regan could see stars out the window. She could see her white puffs of breath shining in the light that wandered in from the distant glow of the streetlights. She could tell from his breathing that Mike was asleep. But Regan didn't sleep for a long time; instead, she lay very still, staring out the window at the bright and distant stars.

Chapter Eight

"WE JUST NEED TO figure out how to get some more heat in here," Mike said. Regan looked around the attic. Somehow, dingy and cold and sad as it was, it had become a kind of home. It was late October, almost November, and getting dark and cold. She and Mike had scrounged old sleeping bags to hang on the windows and over the walls. They had found pieces of carpeting for the floor and even some posters for the walls. They visited places that gave away coats and sleeping bags and warm socks—they even got another mattress. Now they had two mattresses on the floor, side by side. But their only heat came from several candles stuck in a box of sand.

This morning, Regan lifted an edge of the quilt and stared out the window at the grey-dark street. Rain poured down the window, poured off the roof, ran along the side of the street. People hurried by, bent under umbrellas and hats, bundled in scarves and coats, on their way home. The buses and cars splashed through a layer of water. Regan sighed. At least the roof didn't leak. The candles flickered in the corner but it was still cold, so cold. She could never seem to get warm anymore, except in bed, at night.

"Maybe someone will put a fire on downstairs," she said.

"Yeah, maybe."

They had a routine now. Regan had given up trying to go to school. They had divided up Regan's money and figured out what to spend it on. Each morning they went to a coffee shop and stayed as long as they could. Then, if it wasn't raining, Mike went busking and Regan went to the dojo and worked out with Sifu. He had asked her to come in every day to train for the upcoming tournament. He never questioned how or where she was living and she didn't volunteer any information.

Sometimes she stood in line at the food bank. Sometimes she stood in line at other places, wherever they were giving away food. On rainy days, she and Mike sat in the library and read; occasionally they rode around on the buses and wandered in malls and stared at the store windows. Sometimes they lay on the old mattress upstairs in the squat, bundled in layers of sleeping bags and torn quilts, and talked about imaginary futures in which they might live. Always, Regan watched the street for any sign of her mother. Some days she was sure she saw her mother or heard her laugh, but it was never her. And then she would come back to the squat, walk warily in the backdoor, always careful about how much noise she made, and tiptoe up the stairs. She didn't want to talk to the other people in the house.

It was hard to keep track of who lived in the house. People came and went, but almost no one came up the dark stairs to where Regan and Mike had made their quilted room. People came in and out of the back door. When Regan came in, she mostly kept her head down, her face turned away. She didn't want to see or know what people were up to. But sometimes there would be a group of kids sitting around the fireplace and she would look in to see if it was anyone she knew. If someone had scrounged enough firewood, and kept a fire going for a while, the house would warm up. Even the attic would get warm. But there was rarely enough firewood to keep a fire going long enough to really warm the house.

Regan had started bringing home wood as well. She found if she prowled the alleys there were piles of old lumber, or bits of stumps and branches. But it was heavy and wet and it was very hard to carry enough wood to make much of a difference. Often the wood was in long pieces studded with nails. But it was something to do. She piled the wood beside the fireplace and left it to dry.

One night, she and Mike had found a whole carton of

sausages, smokies, and wieners behind one of the stores that they often checked for food. They brought it home and that night, there had been a party of sorts beside the brick fireplace. They had toasted the smokies and wieners and stuffed themselves. People shared cigarettes, wine, and drugs, but Regan left as soon as the drinking started. Mike stayed. She heard him come to bed hours later, but didn't wake up enough to say anything. That morning she went to the coffee shop by herself. She caught up with Mike that afternoon in the small park. He said nothing about the evening before and she didn't ask questions.

Now she turned from the window. Mike was sitting beside the box of lit candles, poking at the dripping wax with his fingers.

"Mike, how long can we do this, just survive like this? Shouldn't we figure out what to do next? What if some developer decides to tear the house down? What would we do?"

"How do I know?"

"But, Mike . . ."

"Regan, you been on the street what, a month? I been here since I was twelve, four years now. You survive how you can, you take what comes, if there's food you eat it and if there's not, you go to sleep. If there's drugs or company for the night you take it because it's there and it'll get you through. You don't know anything. Don't ask me questions like that. I'll get through this winter like I got through all the others, and then maybe in the spring something better will come, maybe someone will come, maybe something will happen. Who knows? Don't ask." He turned his face back to the candles, began passing his finger through the flame and holding it there until he winced from the pain. Then he did it over again.

Regan said nothing. She crawled into the sleeping bag, and turned her face into the pillow; it smelled of mould and must.

"Maybe tomorrow I will stay at Sifu's," she said.

"Whatever."

And then she realized, somewhat to her astonishment, that Mike's shoulders were shaking, that he was trying very hard not to cry.

She got out of the sleeping bag, went and sat beside him.

"What?" she asked.

"There is no we," he said. "I told myself that. I promised myself I'd never trust anyone again, I'd never let me turn into a 'we'. It doesn't work. It's how you get hurt."

"But that's not true," she said. "You're my friend. I'm your friend."

"And you'll go somewhere," Mike said. "You'll get tired of this crap and go, to your grandmother's or somewhere, or a care home. And you'll be gone. That's what people do, they leave. Or I leave. That's how it works."

"Not for me," Regan said. "I'll wait for my mom. I'll find her or she'll find me, somehow. I don't care how long it takes. I just know. I know she's coming back. And when she does come back, and we have a home again, you can come with us. I'll always be your friend. I don't leave people."

"You're crazy."

"No, I'm not."

"What if your mom doesn't come back?"

"She will. I know she will."

"How can you believe that?"

Regan thought for a while. Then she said, "Once, when I was little, I was learning to swim. We were at my grandmother's place. There's a beach there. My mom was holding me in the water and then she said, 'Okay, Regan, I want you to try to swim on your own.' I was scared. And my mom said, 'If you feel you can do it, then you can. If you can see yourself doing it, then you can. Just trust yourself.' And I thought about it. And then I knew I could swim and I did. I just took off and swam by myself. It's the same feeling now. I just know she's coming back. Somehow. I know. I'm going to believe it. Because if I can see it, it's going to happen."

Mike said nothing. They sat together, watching the candle flames flicker and dance, feeling the small amount of warmth they gave off. Mike stood up, got a blanket, sat down and draped it around both their shoulders. Regan didn't remember falling asleep but when she woke in the morning, she was tucked in her sleeping bag and Mike was gone. A tiny note on his sleeping bag read, "Gone hunting. Back when I find something. You deserve better."

Regan hugged the sleeping bag to her shoulders and read the note again. She wasn't really sure what it meant, but it was pretty clear that Mike had left her here alone. And that was the last thing she wanted. Panic rose from her belly into her throat. She didn't want to be alone anymore, not in this cold damp house, in this wet rainy city. She pulled the sleeping bag around her shoulders, put her face on her knees, wrapped her arms around her knees, and rocked back and forth as fear surged through her. No, she couldn't sit still, she had to move, she had to do something, go look for Mike, maybe she should get some food first.

She counted the stash of money; there was depressingly little left, forty dollars and some change. It had gone fast. Mike made money busking but Regan didn't know where to get more money. She could ask her grandmother again, but that would mean explaining how desperate things had become. She kept rocking, thinking, rocking.

Finally the fear relented enough so that she could move, stretch. Her body ached and her teeth hurt. She needed warmth, food. She pulled on as many layers of clothes as she could, pulled on her backpack, and crept downstairs. She tiptoed by the dusty room that had once been a living room. It was a chaos of old chairs, torn pieces of carpet, bottles, garbage bags, and a couple of sagging, grimy sofas. This morning there was someone wrapped in a sleeping bag snoring on one of the sofas. A brindle-coated, sad-faced dog lay beside the couch. When Regan stopped, the dog lifted its head and its tail thumped on the floor. Regan hesitated. She liked dogs. She'd always wanted one. But she didn't know anything about them. This one looked thin. It had a massive black leather collar around its neck.

"Hey, dog," she whispered. Its ears perked but then it dropped its head onto the floor again. Maybe the dog would be there when she got back and she could try to get to know it better. She could bring it a treat of some kind.

She went to her favourite coffee shop and paid at the counter for a coffee and a bagel stuffed with cheese and bacon. She counted her money again as she went to a booth, even the pennies. Then she pulled out the laptop and checked her email. There were rarely any personal messages just for her; there were listserv messages from Sifu, messages from her school, messages from Facebook from people she didn't remember and didn't care about. These felt like ghost messages from a world she had once lived in and cared about, but no longer. She read through them quickly, looked through some music sites and closed the computer. Nothing seemed interesting this morning, and she felt too exposed, sitting in the coffee shop by herself when she had come here so often with Mike.

The owner nodded to her as she left, and now she had to figure out how to fill the rest of the day, how to keep warm, how to find food, and how to keep the panic that was still gnawing at her belly from taking over. She spent part of the morning in the library, but nothing in the books interested her. At noon, she stood in line for an hour at one of the churches that offered a free lunch. It was raining and the lineup seemed unusually long. By the time she got inside, she was soaked and shivering and the bowl of lukewarm canned vegetable soup and the stale white bun didn't help much.

After lunch, she decided to go back to the squat. At least she could curl up in her sleeping bag and try to get warm. It was still raining hard and she ran the last few blocks. She ducked down the alley and in through the back door and stopped. To her surprise, it was warm. She came in through the ruined kitchen to the living room. An electric heater was blasting heat into the room. The man with the dog was sitting beside it.

"Wow," she said. "How did you do that?"

"Ran a line from the power pole next door. Stole an extension cord from the neighbour's back porch. Hooked it up."

"That's amazing. It's almost warm in here."

"Yeah, come and get dry," he said. "You look like a soaked puppy."

She hesitated, but the warmth drew her in. She sank to the floor in front of the heater. Warmth. It felt so good. She stretched out her hands. The dog raised its head and watched her. It had sad, dark eyes.

"What's your dog's name?" she asked.

"Joe, just plain old Joe."

"Hey, Joe," she said to the dog. And then to the man. "Can I pet him?"

"Yeah, sure, hold out your hand, let him get used to you. He's kinda protective sometimes."

The dog sniffed her hand, and then she patted its head. The dog lay down and stretched its length on the floor. She scratched its head and belly and when she stopped the dog licked her hand and then lay back down with a deep sigh.

"Oh, I forgot, I was going to bring him a treat."

"Yeah, he ain't eaten in a couple of days. I can get food for me, pretty much, but gettin' food for the dog is a lot tougher. I been thinking I should let him go, maybe let the SPCA folks have him. But they'd probably just put him down and I'm kind of attached to the dude."

"Where did you get him?"

"Oh, some idiot had a bunch of puppies he couldn't look after. I took this one. He's still young, still learnin'. I like dogs, always had dogs, once."

"You had dogs? Where?"

"On a farm, out in the valley. Grew up there. Had collies, cattle dogs. Long time ago now. But it's kinda stupid to have a dog in the city when I can't even handle looking after my own self. Hey, Joe? Ain't that right?"

The dog wagged its tail but didn't get up. Regan was secretly shocked. How could someone have a dog and not feed it?

"Maybe I can find him something," she said. "I'll look around. There might be something behind one of the grocery stores." She didn't even know what dogs ate. Dog food? Right. It came in cans or bags. She'd seen it in the grocery store. Weren't there some of the food places that gave out dog food? Hadn't she seen a notice on a bulletin board somewhere? Right, the church. There was a notice there. It didn't say dog food, it just said, "Help is here for any and all kinds of stuff, if you need it." Kind of an odd notice. She had no idea what it meant but she could ask. Even if they didn't give out dog food, they might know where she could find some.

She got up to go. "I think the church down the street might know where I could get some."

"Yeah, sure," the guy said. "So, you gotta boyfriend?" he asked.

"Yeah," said Regan. She hesitated, flustered by the question. She'd never thought of Mike as her boyfriend but it felt safer to say he was. "He's busking right now. He'll be back soon. I'd better go." She headed towards the stairs, and then hesitated. She couldn't stand the thought of the dog going hungry. She knew too well what hunger felt like. She sure didn't want to go back out in the rain. But at least she could go check out the church. They might know. She turned around and headed out the back door, ran through the still-drenching rain to the church. At the back of the church a man in a suit and tie was just locking the door.

"Excuse me," Regan said.

"Oh, hi there," the man replied. He smiled. "Can I help you? Hey, come on inside. I was leaving for the day but there's no point in standing out here in the rain." He had a lovely Irish accent. He turned and unlocked the door and held it open for her. Inside was a desk, an office, and beyond, Regan could see a storeroom.

"Do you have any dog food?" she asked.

"Dog food." He sighed. "Do you have a dog?"

"No, there's this guy at my house. He has a dog. He says it hasn't eaten for a couple of days. It didn't look as if he cared much."

The man sighed again. "Aye, poor dogs. They are so faithful and they don't understand neglect. Yes, we have dog food. I'm not supposed to give it out unless I see the actual dog, but you have an honest face and I am going to trust you. Just hold on a moment." He went in the back room and came out with a sack of dry dog food and a bag with four cans inside. "When you feed him, put a little hot water with the food. Makes it taste better."

Regan hesitated. "We don't really have hot water."

"Right," said the man. "Listen, do you want a cup of tea? I was going to go out for my tea because it is just too sad to sit here by myself and drink tea and listen to it rain, but now that you are here, we could have a bit of tea together."

Regan really didn't want tea but she did want some food and to get warm so she followed him to the back. She didn't quite trust the guy. He was far too friendly. People who worked in the various shelters and food stations downtown were friendly enough, but they always had an edgy wariness, as if they had been asked for too many favours, too many times. Guys who were too friendly usually either wanted to talk about religion, or they wanted to ask for money or sex or drugs.

"I'll turn the heater up high, shall I? And I am sure that Father John left a bit of cake around somewhere." He opened the desk drawer. "Ah, yes, apple cake it is."

Regan sat on the edge the chair in front of the desk while he busied himself with a kettle, a teapot, and two mugs. He cut several large pieces of cake, put them on a plate and set it in front of her. Then he poured a mug full of tea, put some milk and sugar on the desk, and handed the mug to her.

"By the way, my name is Reg," he said.

"Mine is Regan."

"No, really?" he turned to face her, laughing. "Are we twins then? That's lovely. I don't think I have ever met a Regan in Canada before. That's an Irish name."

"My mom said it means 'queen.'"

"And so it does, indeed."

Regan held the hot teacup with both hands, letting the heat warm her numb wet fingers. She was trying to stifle the urge to grab the cake and stuff it in her mouth. As Reg went on talking, she put the mug down, grabbed a piece of cake, and wolfed it down in two bites.

"I think I've seen you around a few times," he said now. "Do you live near here?"

"A few blocks away," Regan said. She wasn't about to tell this strange man anything despite his too-friendly smile and his charming accent.

"You know, people say this is a terrible neighbourhood," he went on, "and I haven't been here that long, but I find people here rather kind. Look at you now, coming out in the pouring rain, just to get a wee doggie some food. I see people all the time, looking out for each other, trying to help out. Do you find that?"

"Sometimes," Regan said. Any moment now, she thought, he's going to start going on about whether I go to church or school or where I live. She had finished all the cake and the tea and was thinking of a polite way to get herself out the door with the dog food.

"Ah, I love it here," Reg said. "I love the city and the ocean and those crazy big mountains. Have you ever gone skiing, Regan?"

Skiing! "Nope."

"It's amazing, closest thing to flying there is. And hiking in those mountains. So beautiful. I've been thinking it would be good to start a club of sorts, maybe an outdoors club, take some of the young people down here hiking and camping. What do you think? Would you be part of such a thing?"

"I don't know. I'd have to think about it." Hiking. What did he mean by that?

"Would you like some more tea?"

She shook her head. "Thanks for the cake," she said.

"Anytime, it was lovely to chat. But here's me, running on when you have probably got plenty to do. Good luck with the dog."

"He's not my dog."

"Oh, right, well, I hope it all turns out."

She ducked out the door, back into the rain, tucked the heavy bag of dog food under her coat, and hung the handles of the bag over her arm. Between her backpack, the dog food, and the bag full of cans, she was almost staggering by the time she got to the squat.

When she went inside, the dog stood up, growling. He was tied to a chair. The heater was unplugged. A torn piece of paper was tucked under his collar. She held out her hand to him but he backed away, still growling.

She ripped open the bag of dog food and held a piece of the dry food on her hand. The dog sniffed. He stopped growling. She squatted on her heels in front of him and he crawled towards her. She held the piece of kibble out to him and he took it, very gently from her fingers. She took the piece of paper off his collar.

"Can't keep Joe. Can't feed myself, let alone him. If you don't want him, the SPCA will take him." No signature. She sighed. She fed Joe piece after piece of kibble. He took each piece politely from her fingers. She didn't want to pour it out on the floor and she didn't think there were any dishes in the house. Suddenly, she heard voices in the back yard. She untied the dog, hoisted her backpack, the dog food and the bag of cans, grabbed the dog's leash, and headed for the stairs.

He followed her willingly, and when they were in the attic and the door was closed, she fed him some more dog food. But when she let go of the leash, he went to the door and whimpered. She took the leash and led him downstairs and back out into the rain. He headed immediately for a puddle under a bush and slopped at it desperately. Then he cocked his leg and had a very long pee. She realized he must have been holding it for hours. He probably needed a walk. She led him down the hill and over the railroad tracks to the park beside the ocean and took off the leash. He ran into the dim mist, disappeared, then came back, ran past her, and disappeared again. She kept walking.

The rain had slackened and turned into a kind of dense mist, as though the air itself was made of water. She stared out into the harbour at the bright lights from the ships and the dark water lapping at the steep jagged rocks at the edge of the park. She usually didn't like being outside at night by herself, but now she wasn't by herself. She had this crazy dog, which kept running by her like some kind of insane boomerang. What if he didn't come when she called him? Then what?

But he kept coming back. Once he had a stick in his mouth that he was tossing as if it were a toy. When he dropped it, she picked it up and threw it and he ran after it, picked it up, chewed it, dropped it, and took off running again. Regan kept walking along the sidewalk, past the docks and boats and trains. The dog kept pace with her, kept her in sight, and eventually he calmed down enough to trot along at her side.

When she figured they both had had enough walking, she headed up through the alleys towards the squat. She noted with some amusement that people avoided her and the dog; some people even crossed the street to avoid her. She went in the back door of the squat and headed quickly up the stairs. She could hear loud voices arguing from the front room; something crashed. It sounded like glass breaking. Then someone screamed and someone else kept on swearing. She didn't want to know what it was about. She was chilled through and glad to crawl into the sleeping bag. The dog flopped down beside her with a heavy sigh. She patted his head and he licked her hand.

In middle of the night, she woke up. Someone was pounding on the door of her room, yelling, "Susie, Suze, you in there? Hey, Suze, c'mere. I wanta talk to you." A man's voice. He sounded really drunk.

The dog woke as well. He jumped to his feet and began to bark, a deep menacing bark that rebounded off the walls and echoed around the room.

"Get lost," she yelled. "Or my dog will tear your leg off."

There was silence on the other side of the door, then she heard footsteps pounding, stumbling, back down the stairs.

"Good dog," she said. "Really good dog."

Regan lay back down and the dog snuggled into her side. She couldn't sleep and neither could he. The dog kept his ears perked and occasionally growled low in his throat. They both listened to the noises coming from distant parts of the house, voices yelling, music, swearing. Eventually, the noise dwindled and Regan and Joe both went to sleep.

When Regan woke in the morning, the dog was sitting at the door, looking anxious. Of course, he needed to pee. She shrugged on her jacket, grabbed the backpack, and headed down the stairs. The house was quiet. There were bodies draped on the torn furniture, wrapped in blankets and sleeping bags. Regan took Joe into the garbage-strewn backyard, and then headed down the street to the coffee shop. She looked at the clock and the calendar on the wall. October 23. With a shock, she realized it was her birthday. Some birthday! Fourteen and her life was a disaster.

After buying some breakfast, she had less than twenty dollars left. The sun was shining and she sat outside at a table with the dog, devoured a fruit smoothie and her usual breakfast bagel, throwing the dog some crusts. He snapped them up in mid-air.

Decision time, she thought. She had to do something. She had to get some money. She had to find a better place to live. The guy banging on the door had scared her. The place was basically a drug-party house. The dog had saved her but she didn't know how she could manage to keep the dog and look after him. She couldn't even look after herself. She had to figure out what to do. Mike was gone. She had run out of ideas, options, and energy. The food barely touched the empty cold place inside her. Help, she thought to herself. Help, help, help.

"Hey," said a voice in her ear. "Why, it's my wee cousin, Regan. May I join you? Is this your doggie? What's his name?"

She looked up. There was Reg, grinning at her.

"His name is Joe," Regan said.

Reg squatted down and patted Joe's head, rubbed his ears, then flopped into the chair opposite her. "I'm so glad to run into you. Actually, I was looking for you. I've got an idea. I want to know what you think of it. I've been thinking we need to reach out to the young people on the street; we need to figure out how to network and connect a bit better, I'm thinking maybe a blog would help, maybe we could even text it to people. What do you think? Would you read such a thing?"

"Maybe," she said. Who was this guy and what did he really want?

"And we'd need someone to write it. Can you write, Regan? You've lived down here a while, yes?"

"Yeah, quite a while."

"Do you like to write?"

"I do, yes, actually, I like to write." Jeez, would the guy never go away.

"Would you like to try it? We'd pay you, of course, something anyway. You could work at the church. There's an empty office, well, it's a closet, really, but we could put a table in there, and a chair. What would you need? A computer? A cell phone?"

Regan was so tired. All she really wanted to do was lie down and sleep for a month. When was the last time she had slept a whole night? No, first she wanted a shower, and clean clothes. And then sleep. She could take a shower at Sifu's studio. She could even do laundry there. Perhaps that was what she should do. But what about Joe? Would Sifu let her keep him?

"I don't know what to do about the dog," she said. "I just don't."

"He's a lovely dog." Reg frowned. "He needs a real home."

"Yeah, sure, don't we all."

That came out more bitter than she'd intended but she

was so tired. And nothing Reg said was really making sense. Pay her, to write a blog? Yeah, right.

Reg frowned again. "Hmm. I might know someone who would take him. I'll ask around at church. So what do you think, about the job, I mean? I'm sorry it wouldn't pay much."

"Sure," she said. "I'll come by later." And it would turn out to be a joke, she thought, a prank. Who knew, maybe this guy was some kind of nut, although he didn't seem crazy. He seemed really nice. But how could she tell. She yawned. "I'm sorry," she said. "I didn't get much sleep and I got up early with the dog."

"No problem," he said. "I've got to get to work, anyway. I'll see you later then. Bye Regan, bye Joe."

After he left, Regan and Joe went to Sifu's studio. Sifu already had a class going but Regan left Joe tied to a chair in the office and went and had a shower. She put on her kung fu uniform, then washed her clothes in the washer and dryer in the back, and then found a pile of mats, pulled Joe down to lie beside her, and went to sleep.

Sifu woke her later by waving a steaming carton of chicken soup under her nose. Joe was sitting up, growling low in his throat.

"My best student," he said, "sleeps all day. No time to practise." He was smiling at her.

"Sorry, Sifu." She struggled to sit up, to bow, and to quiet Joe, who was now sniffing at the chicken soup.

"Nice dog," said Sifu.

"Someone left him at my house. He's great but I can't keep him. He's probably hungry."

"Eat soup," said Sifu. "Come practise. Then we'll feed ourselves and the dog."

She gulped down the soup. Sifu had also brought a package of tuna fish sandwiches from a deli. She ate half of them and fed half of them to Joe. Then she put on a white robe, went out to the floor, bowed, and began her practice of kicks, punches, and spins. She worked until she was hot and sweating. Then Sifu came out and they went through their practice again together. When they were done, they bowed to each other.

"Competition is three weeks away," said Sifu. "I have sent in your name. You must practise every day now."

"Sure," said Regan.

"And you need to eat better. From now on, you eat at Don's Deli. Get your food there. My friend will put it on account."

"Wow, thanks."

"And sleep here?"

"Yes," said Regan. "I'll sleep here."

Sifu went out of the office and began working with some other students. Regan changed back into her clean street clothes. She sat in Sifu's office, trying to decide what to do next. Could she believe Reg? Shouldn't she at least check out his offer even if it didn't really make sense? She needed something with which to make a bit of money.

She went back outside, into the rain, and trudged the several blocks to the church. When she came in the door, Reg jumped to his feet. "You came!" he exclaimed. "I didn't know if you believed me. Come on, I'll show you your office."

They went down a hall to a small office with a desk, a chair, a computer, and a basket for Joe to sleep in.

"The blog is all set up," he said. "I've bookmarked it on the computer, I've set you up with a gmail account, and all you need to do is write something. Then I'll take a look at it, maybe do a bit of editing, and then we can start networking it on Facebook and Twitter and all those places. What do you think?"

Regan stared at him. He beamed back at her.

"I've never written stuff for other people," Regan said. "Just in school. What do you want me to write?"

"Well, you live down here, you know the people, the life, the folks here, maybe just stories of what you do day-to-day, how people get by, who you meet, I don't know really. It's just a crazy idea . . . if it doesn't work, we can try something else. Just try it, see what happens. Hang on, I'll bring you some tea and cake for inspiration."

Which he did. And then he left her alone with the computer.

She stared at the blank screen. She checked her email, her Facebook, opened up a blank word document.

What the heck? No one would ever read it. She could write how she felt. She thought about standing in line in the rain for a bun and soup, she thought about sitting in the sun, beside the fire, under the bridge. She thought about the long cold nights in the attic of the squat. And she began to write.

Chapter Nine

EIGHT WEEKS, TWO MONTHS. Regan sat in front of the computer trying to figure out what to write but she was thinking about numbers. Sixty-four days. That's how long her mom had been gone. How many hours, minutes, seconds?

Life almost had a routine now. It was almost bearable except for the great gaping hole in the middle that was her mother's absence. And for the fact that now when she walked down the street, she looked for her mother and she also looked for Mike. And for the fact that when she wrote, sometimes she had to stop and stand up and pace the room until the choking feeling in her throat subsided enough to let her breathe.

The kung fu tournament was now in two weeks. She was practising hard for it. But what was the point if her mom wasn't there to watch?

Sifu had been great. She got her breakfast and morning coffee at the deli and Reg brought her food every day. She slept in the back room at the dojo. It was far too quiet at night but way better than the squat.

She couldn't figure Reg out either. He was endlessly kind, he was always cheerful, and he seemed to think that whatever she wrote was great. He had been true to his word; he found a home for Joe although he still brought him into the office for an occasional visit. When she was there, in the afternoon, he made tea for Regan and brought sandwiches for her along with a seemingly endless supply of cookies and cakes for the office and its stream of visitors. She was never quite sure just what his job description was or what the office was for. It seemed to be a place of last resort: when someone couldn't find what they needed anywhere else, they found their way to this small dimly lit office at the back of the church. He counselled, he listened. He had tea with the priest, Father Dominic, in the afternoon. Reg never mentioned religion. And he never asked Regan about her life, even though she expected him to.

For the first week, she had thought of various smart answers to make when he began preaching about religion. She had asked her mom about religion once.

"Yeah," Regan's mom had said. "I tried that after your dad died. I prayed and I tried and tried to make sense of what had happened to him. Mostly I just wanted to know why it had happened. We were so happy and we had you, and then he was gone. I talked to the minister at church about it but nothing he said made sense either. So, I gave it up. I figured, I'm on my own, and no one seemed to care except your dad's mom and her heart was broken too. So we weren't much comfort to each other."

But Reg didn't hassle her. He corrected any spelling mistakes she made, and then he sent her writing out on various listservs and websites, and amazingly, it got lots of responses.

She had chosen a pen name. "Runner," she called herself. She wasn't a runaway; all she wanted was her home back, but most of the kids on the streets had run away from something, and she thought they might relate. She wrote what she saw and experienced. People standing in the rain to get food. The bottle pickers scrounging through dumpsters. The kids on street corners with dogs. The sound of the rain on the roof of the squat during the nights she had spent there with Mike and then by herself. How it felt when she was practising in the dojo. The satisfying feeling of kicks, punches, falls. She never wrote about her mother or herself. But she wrote about how peaceful and safe she felt walking with Joe, alone in the harbourside park late at night.

But today, no words would show up at all. It was pouring rain outside again and the small room she worked in was stifling hot. Normally, she loved the heat and couldn't get enough of it. She had moved the desk and chair so her back was just above the electric heater on the wall. But today the walls were closing in. There wasn't enough air. She grabbed her jacket and headed outside. She went several blocks to the small park where Mike used to juggle. The park was deserted. No one was sitting outside in the rain; no one was walking dogs or playing with kids. Everyone was in cars or offices. It was late afternoon and the light was already gloomy.

She walked back to her favourite coffee shop and ordered a sandwich and a coffee. The owner, Rob Lam, was cheerful and chatty.

"Great day out there."

"Yeah, lovely," Regan said. She really didn't feel like talking.

But Rob followed her to the booth where she sat with her coffee and ham sandwich.

"So where's your boyfriend these days? Haven't seen him around anywhere."

"He's not my boyfriend. He went travelling."

She had made up various lies to explain Mike's absence. Sometimes she even believed them herself. Despite the coffee and the sandwich, she still felt hollow inside. She left the restaurant and headed back towards the church. She wrapped her arms around herself. Her head felt light and hollow. How long could she go on like this? What was she going to do? Maybe she should just try and accept that her mother was gone, and go back to her grandmother's house. She could look after her grandmother as she got older. She could do some of the cleaning and cooking so she wouldn't be a burden.

And then, at least neither Regan nor her grandmother would be alone. Also, she could go back to school. She had given up on school for now. It was just too much effort to try to keep her life together and do school as well.

When Regan had got back on the bus to return home, her grandmother's face had crumpled like a piece of paper. Her grandmother was trying so hard not to cry. Regan hadn't cried then either. But she did now. She pulled the hood of her jacket over her head. She put her back against the wall of a building, and slid down the wall so she was crouched on the sidewalk. She put her head on her knees. She tried to stifle the sobs but they came out in bubbles and gasps. It was the memory of her grandmother's face that did it.

"Queenie," said a voice in her ear. "Queenie, I think I found something. Maybe."

Mike's voice. Mike's arms around her. She leaned her head on his shoulder and went on sobbing. Maybe it was all a dream but it was a good dream, the first good dream she had had in a while.

Then his words penetrated the fog.

"Found? What, where? Where have you been? What did you find out?"

Regan scrambled to her feet, wiped her eyes and face with her sleeves.

Mike stood up. He was thinner than she remembered. And someone had cut his hair short. His long corkscrew curls were gone.

"It's a long story."

"Come to the church. I've got an office. I'm writing stuff. A blog." The words tumbled out. "We can't talk on the street."

They walked silently, side by side, to the church office, went inside and down the hall to Regan's cubbyhole. Reg was in the back, talking to Father Dominic.

As soon as the door was closed, Regan said, "Talk, talk. Tell me everything."

"I got myself invited to one of those high stakes poker games. I found him. I went along with that guy, Clay, the one we met at the hotel, remember? I had to do some fancy talking to convince him I had forgotten all about you and had no idea where you were. I said you had left town."

Regan nodded.

"These guys all know each other. They're part of a circuit that goes all over North America. Anyway, long story short, we ended up in Vegas. He bought me a fake passport." He closed his eyes for a second. "What a gross place. I saw a lot of crap I would rather not know about. These are not nice people, not nice in any way. Anyway, one night Clay got really drunk. He usually doesn't drink that much and he can't handle it. Anyway, he told me some stuff. He's actually a drug dealer. At least I think he is, from what he said. Regan, I think you're right. Your mom is probably here, in the city, somewhere. Maybe she's hiding, or maybe she's kidnapped. I don't know. But there's these houses run by drug gangs. They keep people there to work—kind of like slaves. Plus they make drugs. They rent big houses out in the suburbs and turn them into drug labs. It's really dangerous."

"What house? Where is it?"

"Look, Regan, there's no way to know if your mom is there or not. And I don't even have an address. But I have an idea. After Clay passed out one night, I went through his phone and emails. I found some emails from a guy that I think might work for him. One of the emails had a house address. It said they were still looking for the money even though they had found "the package," as they called it. I emailed it to my email address. We can get it off your computer. It's a long shot, but we should check it out. At least it's a step forward."

"Yes, but then what do we do? If she is there, how do we get her out?"

"We need the cops."

"They won't believe me. They don't listen to street kids. You know that."

"If we have proof, they've got to listen. Brenda will listen to you."

"How do we get proof?"

"We've got to get into that house."

"How?"

"They deal drugs, right? Obviously, people have to come and go. I'll just pretend to be a buyer. I'll take pictures with the cell. I know the talk. I can do it."

"No, it's too dangerous. She's my mom. Let me go."

"Yeah, like anyone would take you seriously as a drug dealer. You're just a kid."

"So are you." They both stopped.

Someone knocked on the door and Reg stuck his head in. "Just made tea," he said. "And shortbread. Anyone here like shortbread?" They both stared at him without answering.

"And you would be?" He stared at Mike.

"Oh, I'm Mike. I'm a friend of Regan's. We were just, umm, talking."

Regan nodded.

"Okay, well, tea's ready."

Reg shut the door.

"Who the heck was that?" Mike asked.

"That's Reg. He works here. He helps people. He gave me some dog food after a drunk left his poor dog at the squat. Then he asked me to write a blog for street kids. At first, I thought he was some religious nut, but he's really nice. He doesn't preach or ask questions. So far."

"I could use some tea," Mike said. "I haven't slept much."

"Mike . . ." Regan said and then stopped.

"Yes?"

"Umm, I—well, I missed you. I couldn't stay at the squat when you were gone. It was too weird. Some drunk banged on the door one night. I was lucky I had the dog, Joe, with me that night."

"Regan," Mike said. His face twisted. "Yes, I missed you too. Just leave it at that, okay. C'mon, we'll have some tea with the dude. It might help us think."

They went to the outer office. Reg poured tea, set out milk, sugar, and cookies.

"Mike, have you read Regan's blog? She's getting many comments on it. Lots of people reading it. She's quite the lovely writer."

"Nope, haven't seen it."

"So, Mike, do you live around here as well."

"I don't have an answer for that, Reg, I don't really live anywhere at all," Mike said. His voice was soft and slow. "If there's a bed, I sleep, and if there's food, I eat. Some days I juggle. Some days I just sit out in the rain."

"I see." Reg frowned. "Doesn't sound too healthy."

Regan looked back and forth at the two guys. She could almost see the hostile sparks going back and forth.

"Well, you know, we think very highly of Regan and her work. Very highly indeed," Reg said.

"That's nice. Nice she has a place to get out of the rain occasionally."

"It's a real job," Reg said. "We're paying her and she is doing very good work. I'm going to be quoting some of the people in the forums in my dissertation."

"Your dissertation?" Regan asked.

"Well, yes, I am doing research work down here, on street youth. This way I have access to some of them without having to track them down on the street. Of course I am doing in-person interviews as well."

"You're a student?"

"Yes, transferred here, actually, from Dublin."

"You never mentioned this," Regan said.

"Oh, didn't I? I thought you knew. I thought I explained it to you. Oh well," Reg continued, "any questions you have, just fire away. I am trying to find out how much street youth can access social services and how such access can better be improved. It seems to me a lot more could be done."

Regan sat back. Of course, it all made sense now. Helping people was also a way of getting them to talk. Reg was just another person using the street people to get something.

"So, after you leave here, you get to go off and be a professor of something, is that right?" Mike asked.

"Well, I'll be looking for a job, certainly."

"And you can forget all about your days slumming it down here in the crap. And Regan and I can just get on with our happy lives. Did you know her mom disappeared two months ago and she's been on the street ever since? Did you interview her about that? Or about sleeping in a squat with drunks trying to break down the door?"

"No, I didn't know. That's terrible! Regan, why didn't you tell me?"

Regan looked at Reg and Mike. "I didn't tell you because you never asked. And this is stupid, sitting here arguing. All I want to do is find my mom. Mike thinks he knows where she is. I don't care about your dissertation or your research or whatever it is. None of it will make a difference to me. What I need is to figure out how to make the cops believe me."

"Why wouldn't they believe you?" Reg asked.

"I'm a kid, a street kid. Cops don't listen to street kids.

They'll just assume my mom ran away for fun and I'm on drugs or whatever."

"Oh, I see."

"You're the one doing the research," Mike said. "Haven't you noticed how polite and respectful the cops are with kids down here?"

"Yeah, you're right. Sorry. Look, if there's anything I can do to help, I would be glad to. Maybe I could talk to the cops."

"And tell them what?" Mike asked. "Anyways, thanks for tea but we have stuff we need to figure out. C'mon, Regan."

"Look, I'm sorry, Mike. We seem to have gotten off on the wrong foot here. I really, really do want to help. There must be something I can do. Regan really is a terrific kid."

Mike and Regan stopped on their way out the door.

"Just let me try. I'll come with you to the police. I'm pretty good at talking to people," Reg said.

"That's right, he is," Regan said. "I've seen him in action."

"Is there anyone else can vouch for you? Or who knew your mom, and that the cops would believe?" Reg asked.

"There's Sifu," Regan said. "My kung fu teacher. He thought my mom was great. He told Brenda, this one cop, that she should listen to me. She's his student so she trusts him."

"Great. Let's talk to him first. We'll plan out exactly what to say. Then we can all go together."

Reg locked the office and the three of them went to Sifu's dojo. He was teaching a class but when he saw the three of them come in, he dismissed the class and came over to them.

He wiped his face on a towel; he and Regan bowed to each other.

Reg stuck out his hand. "Reg McDermid here," he said. "I'm a friend of Regan's. She's been working for me, writing a blog."

Instead of shaking Reg's hand, Sifu bowed and after a second, Reg bowed back.

"Mike," said Sifu, turning to Mike.

Mike nodded. "Hey, Sifu," he said.

"Mike thinks he might have an idea about where Regan's mom is," Reg said. "Or at least what happened to her. We're trying to come up with a strategic plan with which to approach the police and convince them that Regan and Mike are credible spokespersons. Regan seems to think they won't listen to her."

"Come to office," Sifu said.

They followed him into his small office, and waited while Sifu arranged chairs. Then he looked at Mike. "You talk first," he said.

Mike told his story, starting with Regan and continuing straight through to his adventures with Clay. Several times Reg started to interrupt and Sifu held up a warning hand. When Mike was done, Sifu turned to Regan. "Okay, now, you talk."

Regan sighed. She launched into the whole story, starting with the moment her mom walked out of their apartment and ending with meeting Mike on the street an hour earlier.

When she was silent, Sifu turned to Reg. "So why are you here?"

"Well," Reg began stiffly. "I am actually a graduate student, doing research work on street youth. I thought asking Regan to write a blog and setting up a forum would be a great way to contact street youth."

"Did she know this is what you were doing?"

Reg hesitated. "Well, I didn't really explain it clearly enough, perhaps."

Sifu just looked at Reg whose face turned an interesting shade of pink.

"Many people study, much writing, many reports, nothing changes," he said, and shrugged. He turned to Regan. "What do you wish to do? What do you need from us?"

Regan hesitated. What she wanted to say was, let's go to that house Mike told me about, smash it to bits, and get my mom back. But she knew that wasn't what Sifu was asking. And if her mom wasn't there, then smashing things would not achieve much.

"That policewoman, Brenda, I don't think she really listened to me even after you talked to her. I think she thought my mom had just run away and left me alone. She seemed to think anyone who lived in this part of town was probably a bad mom or a prostitute or an idiot. She told me I should go live with my grandma. I don't know if the cops ever really looked for my mother."

"So, we will convince them," Sifu said cheerfully. "They are just humans, make mistakes, get things wrong, need more information, new information. You, Reg, are a writer, yes? You can write all this down, make a report that will actually be good for something. Police like reports. Are you a doctor yet?"

"Well, almost."

"Good, you are now Dr. McDermid, researcher, friend of Regan, investigator, university prof. Go write report. Two hours, and then we send it to Brenda, then we go meet with her, then we make a plan. Brenda is a good person. I will talk to her. You," he said to Regan. "Go practise. Mike, go shower, eat, and sleep in that order."

Regan put on her outfit. She punched, kicked, fell, rolled, and when she was breathing hard, Sifu brought her staff, and she went through her routine again, until she was exhausted, panting, soaked in sweat. But she kept her back straight, kept her moves controlled and smooth.

"Good," said Sifu. "Go, shower, change, then bring computer."

She met him in his small office about the time Reg showed up and Mike woke up. All four of them studied the printed copies of the report that Reg had made. Regan was impressed. It was precise, clear, and factual. She and Mike suggested a few small changes and then Regan put in the USB hard drive Reg had given her, downloaded the report, and emailed it to the address on the card Brenda had left with her.

"You phone her now," Sifu said. "Tell her to read the report and call you back."

Brenda wasn't there. Regan left her a message, asked her to call at Sifu's number, hung up the phone. "Now what?" she asked.

"Now, we eat," said Sifu cheerfully. "We order in. Chinese, Greek, Thai, sushi?"

"I'm not hungry," Regan said.

"Doesn't matter," Sifu said. "Warriors must eat. You stay strong, stay centred."

Regan could have killed him for his cheerfulness. But when the food came, she discovered she was hungry.

While they were eating, the phone rang. Sifu answered. "Yes," he said, "she is here." He handed the phone to Regan.

"Regan," Brenda's voice sounded in her ear, brisk and professional. "So I read your report. Sounds like you and I have some things to talk about. Can you come over here?"

"When?"

"Right now."

"Can I bring my friends?"

"What kind of friends?"

"People who are helping me. Dr. McDermid, who wrote that report. Mike, who found my mom. My sifu, Lee Kwan, who has been taking care of me. The people who have really, actually helped me." She heard her voice rising and she didn't care.

"Tell you what," Brenda said. "Why don't I come over there? Then we can all meet, get to know one another a bit, and you can fill me in. Might be a bit nicer than the police station."

"I think that's a really good idea," Regan said.

"Be right there." She hung up the phone.

"She's coming over," Regan said.

"Good," Sifu said. "Still some food left. Who wants tea?"

It seemed to take Brenda only a few minutes to arrive. She had another cop with her, a tall older man. Their presence changed the room. They weren't smiling when they came in. They refused Sifu's offers of tea or food. They didn't even sit down, just stood towering in the middle of the room.

"This is my partner, Ben Foster," said Brenda. "I've told him as much as I know. As I told you before, we're doing what we can. But, Regan, just because you've managed to convince your friends here of your story, it doesn't give us enough reasons to go raid some house somewhere. We need some actual evidence. I feel very sorry for your loss, but there is a limit to what we can do here."

Regan opened her mouth to speak but no words came out. And then she didn't have to say anything because Sifu took over.

"Yes, and we are so happy you have both come here to listen to Regan and Mike. Regan is very smart, very capable, going to be in the tournament, probably will win. Her mother was also a very good woman, good mother, hard working, looked after Regan very well. She would never abandon her. I know her since she moved here."

"And Regan has been working for me as a research assistant," said Reg. "She is a most capable young woman and I believe her story. I teach at the university and I am here doing doctoral research. Regan's help has been invaluable. She is clearly an honest and straightforward person."

"Okay, okay, so you've got your cheering section going," Brenda said. "What about this young man? He's been in a few scrapes with the cops. I know that. The only real evidence, if I read your report correctly, comes from him. So, Mike? Is that your real name? Even if I believe that Regan's mom is in trouble somewhere, somehow, why should I believe your idea that she is locked up in some meth lab somewhere?"

Again, Sifu intervened. "I know this young man too. He's a good person. I trust him. I believe him. And you, Miss Brenda, you are also a good person. We all want the best thing to happen, for Regan's mom to come home, be safe, Regan and her mom together, at home. How do we make that happen?" Sifu beamed at all of them, as if they were all his best friends just there to have a good time.

And then Ben, the other cop, who had been silent until now, said, "We'd need some grounds to get a search warrant to get into the house. If we have enough reason to believe there's a crime going on, that could do it. Mike, just how certain are you about what you heard?"

"I wasn't drunk or stoned, if that's what you're asking. I pretended to be, but I wasn't. And I told you, I got the address from an email on his computer."

"But you have no way of knowing if this address is where Regan's mom is being held."

"Yeah, that's true."

"But no reason why we can't swing by and check it out," Ben said, turning to Brenda. "We can at least ask questions, talk to the neighbours. If they'll talk to us. Depends on the neighbourhood."

"I want to come too," Regan said.

"Kid, you got our attention, okay," Ben said. "Now let us handle this part. Dealing with these guys is no job for kids. They're nasty and they hurt people."

"But I'll know, I'll know if my mom is there."

"Oh, and how will you know?"

"I just will."

Ben sighed. "Look, we're going to go right now and at least have a look around. We can do that much without having to convince our boss we're not on some crazy wild goose chase, and we'll call you if we find anything. Stay put."

He and Brenda stomped out of the room. The whole studio seemed quieter after they left.

"My, my," said Reg. "That was interesting. Well, must fly, I have a meeting at the university tonight. Here's my cell number if you need me for anything."

He hurried out of the room.

"Very nice man," Sifu said. "But not good for his research to get too involved with research material."

"What?" asked Regan

"He means the university won't like it if he gets too involved with his research subjects. That would be us, especially us with cops," said Mike. "Might make him look bad."

"But I thought he was a nice guy."

"Yes, very kind," said Sifu. "But soon will have important

job and lots of money. Will remember us sometimes. Maybe email occasionally. He means only the best."

Regan nodded. It made sense. Who would want to stay in this neighbourhood when they had a big job and lots of money?

"Now what do we do?" she asked.

"I'm out of here," Mike said. "I got stuff to do." He grabbed his backpack, and disappeared out the door. Regan stared after him. She looked at Sifu. He shrugged, raised his eyebrows.

"Wait, Mike," she called. She ran out the door and into the studio but Mike had already disappeared out the front door of the building. She ran across the studio, pulled open the heavy outside door. Mike was already halfway down the block, walking fast, his head down, his hood pulled over his head.

"Mike." Regan ran after him. Even when she reached him, he didn't look up, just kept on walking. "Where are you going?"

He didn't answer.

"Mike, are you going back to the squat?"

He hunched his shoulders up around his ears and walked faster. Regan had to trot to keep up. "What's the matter?"

He stopped, swung around. "I hate cops," he said. "I could barely stay in that room. All I wanted to do was run."

"Why, what's wrong."

"Do you really want to know?"

"Yes, I do, I really want to know."

"The cops killed my dad," he said. "Or at least, I think they did. The last time I saw him, I was ten years old. It was the middle of the night and I was looking out the window, watching for him. He was coming home from a party. He was late, and drunk. I guess he'd done something, who knows what. Run a red light, something stupid. He was an idiot when he was drunk. Anyway, he got out of his car, and the cops pulled up behind him. They grabbed him, threw him in the cruiser, took him down to the police station. I woke my mom up. I was crying because I was so scared. She went down there right away, but by the time she got there, he was dead. He got into a fight with a cop and the cop shot him. No one knew what really happened. There was some kind of investigation. Nothing happened. My mom fell apart, started drinking. After a couple years, I couldn't take it anymore. I stole some money, hopped a bus, came down here. Now all I want to do is get out of here but I don't know how. I got nowhere to go."

"Can't you go find your mom?"

"Yeah, maybe. I don't know. I think about it all the time. But there's nothing at home for me. My mom's probably still drinking. I want a life. I want to do something with myself. But how do I do that? I can't figure it out. So I just go party instead. God, I'm just like them. And all I ever wanted was to be different."

He pulled his hood down and covered his face.

"What about Reg?"

"What about him?"

"He's smart, he knows about school, why don't you talk to him?"

Mike pulled his hands away so she could see his face. His eyes were red and tears still streaked his cheeks.

"You heard what Sifu said. He doesn't care about people like us."

"Well, he didn't really say that. I think he just said Reg would move on when he finished his research. Why wouldn't he? Why would he want to stay down here? Nobody's here because they like it. And so what? You just need information, right?"

"He'll just think I'm stupid. He's gonna be a university professor. I'm sixteen, dropped out of school, don't know much about anything."

"He's not like that," Regan said. "I sit and listen to him when I'm writing. He treats everybody the same. He seems to like everyone. He's weird that way. Besides, what do you care what he thinks?"

Mike didn't answer.

"Look, I'll go with you." Regan went on, after a moment. "We'll go tomorrow. It's your life. Now come back to the dojo. All your stuff is there. I moved it over from the squat. I'll tell Sifu you have to stay there. We'll eat some more, we'll rest, and we'll wait to hear what the cops say. You don't have to talk to them anymore. I'll do that."

Mike sighed. "God, I'm so tired. Yeah, all right. For tonight. For now." They turned and began walking back to the dojo. Regan looped her arm through Mike's and he gave her half a smile.

"You," he said. "You're crazy. You never give up, do you?"

Regan shook her head. She thought about those dark moments when she had almost given up. "Not yet," she said.

Chapter Ten

"WAITING MAKES YOU crazy," Regan said. She and Mike were sitting in Reg's office. Reg was, as usual, making tea. He didn't seem to be able to do anything without a cup of tea at his elbow.

"Did you call Brenda?" Mike asked.

"Yeah, she said they're watching the house but they're being careful. They don't want to scare these guys and have them move. They're pretty sure it is a drug lab of some kind."

"That makes sense, I guess. So they still don't really know anything?"

"Nope."

"Frickin' cops."

"They're trying."

"Yeah, right."

Reg came in with the tea, and slices of cake on a plate, chocolate this time, and sat down at his desk. He poured the tea, passed the cake.

"So, Mike, how can I help you? By the way, I thought you were absolutely tremendously brave yesterday. Very impressive. I think you made the police take you seriously."

"I did?" Mike sat up straighter in his chair.

"Yes, indeed. You are a bright and intrepid young man."

Mike slumped back down again. "Yeah, with no education and no future, you mean."

"Would you like to go to school?" Reg asked. "Is that something you've thought about?"

"Thought about it, yeah, but I'm not going to sit in some classroom somewhere when I have to hustle just to stay alive."

"Hmm." Reg sat back, tapped his fingers on the desk. "There are university classes at the community centre. Philosophy, English, things like that. Anyone can take them. It's run by the university. People volunteer to teach the classes."

"Yeah, I didn't even finish grade seven. How am I supposed to understand anything they're talking about?"

"Is there anything in particular you want to learn about?"

"Well, when I go the library . . ." Mike hesitated. His face turned red. He pulled his hood up over his head. "I like to read lots of stuff. Mostly I read about history, politics, stuff like that."

"Okay," said Reg. "There is an introductory history course. A friend of mine teaches it. You can borrow the books from the community centre and use the computers there. I'll talk to him if you want."

"I don't know," Mike said. "What good is a history course? It won't get me a job, will it? It won't keep me warm or dry or fed, will it?"

"It certainly won't," Reg said cheerfully. "It's for your mind. You can try it. If you don't like it, you try something else. Part of going to school is figuring out what to study. It took me ages to figure out what I wanted to learn. I tried everything first, even a year on a sheep farm in Australia." He laughed. "My parents were not impressed."

"You have parents?" Mike asked.

"Yes," Reg sighed. "Lovely parents, caring, sincere, sympathetic parents. They phone every week to see if I'm coming home, if I've met someone I like, if I've finally got a real job."

"Wow, parents. So why are you down here then hanging out with us grubbies?"

"Well," said Reg. "Mostly I guess, because I like it here. I like the people, I like the work, I find it interesting. Every once in a while, I even figure something out that might help some people. And then I write letters and grant applications trying to get money for more programs for people here."

"Sifu says you'll just get a job and forget about us," Regan said.

"Did he now?" Reg said. "Oh dear. Well, it would be nice

to get a job." He frowned. Then he laughed. "But forget you two? Not a chance. By the way, Regan, one of the local magazine editors called me about your blog. He's wondering if he can put some of your pieces on his website."

"Really? I mean, wow, well, sure, I guess."

"Take a look at the website first before you decide. I think the editor sent you an email. You'd get a lot of new readers, that's for sure."

"Cool," Regan said.

"And Mike, I'm going to call my friend that teaches the history course. He's at the community centre right now, if you want to go talk to him. You don't have to commit to anything, just have a chat."

Mike looked at Regan. "Okay," he said. "Maybe I'll give it a shot." He pulled his hood down over his forehead and slouched out of the office.

Regan went to her own office and turned on the laptop. Just as Reg had promised, there was an email from an online newspaper editor, asking if he could re-publish some of her blogs. He wanted her to do some re-writing, make them longer, and add some more information. He also asked if she had any new pieces that hadn't been published. Regan twisted her hair around her fingers, stared out the window. What should she say to a real editor, a real writer? Someone who knew about good writing? But he had asked her. Maybe all she had to do was say yes. And then get writing.

She bent over the computer. She needed an idea for a new

piece. She had written about the squat, about lying on the mould-stinking mattress with Joe at her side, the drunk pounding on the door. She had done another piece about walking in the dark, wild park with Joe at her side and the lights of the harbour shining over the black water. She wanted to write about Mike and that brief flash of hope in his eyes when Reg talked about the university courses. She wanted to write about hope, about how important it was, and how even small bits of hope could keep someone going. She began typing, her fingers flying over the keys.

She finished the piece and emailed it to the editor, then sat back, her stomach in knots. Would it come straight back with some nasty remark attached? What did editors actually do, anyway? She heard the phone ring in Reg's office but paid no attention. His phone rang all the time. People constantly came in the door. Tea and cookies and sandwiches were always there. Regan could never quite figure out how people found Reg. He didn't advertise and he didn't really do much, but he seemed to have some kind of magic touch when it came to solving problems for people. Somehow, in the few months he had lived in the neighbourhood, he had gotten to know all kinds of people. He talked to everyone, he talked to waitresses and store owners and people on the streets. She had even seen him once, sitting on the pavement at a corner with a whole group of bottle guys, sitting in a circle, laughing about something.

But now Reg appeared in her door, holding out the phone.

"Regan, it's Brenda," he said. Regan grabbed the phone.

"Hey Regan, it's Brenda, just wanted to give you an update. We've been watching the house, and definitely something is up with these guys. There's traffic coming and going all day and all night. We have to be really, really, careful though. There's dogs in the yard, cameras on all the corners of the house, someone looking out all the time. We've talked to the neighbours. They're scared and they didn't want to talk to us, but they would also really like these guys to be gone. So you were right; these are bad guys. It's a big house, three stories, lots of room to hide people. But we still don't have any reason to go in or get a search warrant or arrest anyone. Unfortunately. No sign of your mom, but that doesn't mean anything. So we're kicking around ideas. We might try to get someone inside but that requires the guys higher up the ladder to give us the okay. That's about all I can tell you for now. Sorry, kid. Wish we could do better."

"But . . ." Regan started.

"Sorry, kid, gotta go, something is happening." The phone clicked in her ear. She stared at the phone and then handed it back to Reg, who was still standing in the doorway.

Regan repeated to Reg what Brenda had said, almost word for word. Then the fear caught her. She stumbled towards Reg, he opened his arms and she put her head on his shoulder and held on tight. He patted her gently on the back.

Finally, she pushed herself away. "What am I going to do? There has to be something I can do. My mom is in danger. I want to help her and all I can do is sit here and write stupid junk on this stupid computer. Why is this happening? All my mom wanted to do was make some money so we could buy some new stuff." Regan was yelling now. "It's not fair. It's so not fair. What did she ever do wrong?"

Reg just let her yell. Finally, when she stopped, he nodded.

"Yes, it is completely unfair and rotten and stupid and every horrible rotten thing you can say about it. All true. Nothing fair about any of it."

Regan slumped back into her chair and covered her face with her hands. Reg brought her some tea and cookies on a plate.

"It's my Irish solution," he said. "A cup of tea in every crisis. Lots of sugar. Fights the shock, helps you think."

Regan didn't want tea but she was shivering with cold. Somehow the hot sweet tea went down to her centre and helped her stop shaking. She took a bite of the cookie Reg was holding out to her. That helped too.

"I want to go out there. I want to see."

"Absolutely not." Reg actually looked shocked. "That's the last place you should be."

"I want to know what my mom is going through. I want to be with her, somehow, even if it's just driving by. I have to see what's going on."

"Regan, you have to let the cops do their job. They are the experts here. They know what they are doing. You can't help. You can't do anything now but wait."

Regan looked at him. "I wrote a new piece," she said. "I sent it to that newspaper dude. I'm going out."

She left the office before Reg could say anything more. She wanted to find Mike but he wasn't at his usual place at the park. She wandered for a long time, downtown, through the crowds of lost kids and panhandlers and drug dealers and business workers and shoppers and tourists and bike couriers and delivery truck drivers. She went by the brightly lit windows of the department stores, past the music stores, the used bookstores, the coffee shops, down to the harbour, and along the walk that led past the water. She walked swiftly, almost wildly. She wanted to yell at the people walking by, some strolling with their dogs, some on bikes, but she knew what happened when you yelled. Everyone ignored you.

Not long after she and her mom had moved to the city, she had seen some young guy standing on the street corner, screaming and sobbing, "Help me, help me," while the crowds that had just been let out from the movie theatres flowed past him, on their way to cars and buses and home. She had wanted to stop but her mom pulled her away, and even then Regan kept looking back. She often wondered what had happened to him. She remembered his face, his long blond hair. Why was he there? What did he want? What did he need help with? Why didn't anyone stop?

It was getting spooky being down here by the ocean in the gathering dark. She headed back up the hill. Her backpack and computer were in Reg's office. At least she could see if she had received an answer from the editor. She began to jog.

As she got near to the old church, she saw Reg standing in the doorway. His face looked worried.

"Regan, I'm so glad you're here. Brenda called again. Something's up."

"What?"

"She just said there'd been an incident of some kind and then I heard something on the radio about a shooting. It sounded as if it might be the same place."

Regan stopped. She felt dizzy. She felt as if a strong wind was going to pick her up and whirl her away.

"What should I do?" she asked.

"You can't do anything. You have to wait."

"I'm not waiting," she shouted. "I'm going out there."

She turned and then remembered that she needed her computer. She dodged around Reg, ran into the office, and opened her laptop. There was an email from the newspaper editor but she didn't stop to read it. Instead, she plugged the address of the house from Mike's email into Google Maps, and then looked at the transit system. She could get there. She'd just have to walk a long ways. She shut down the computer, and headed out of the office.

Reg was standing by his desk. "Regan, wait," he said. "Where are you going?"

"Out there."

She turned and headed out the door and down the street. Reg came pounding behind her. "No, Regan, wait. Come and talk to me."

"No," she yelled over her shoulder.

"Look, I'll get a car," he said. "I'll take you."

She stopped, turned around.

"You have a car?"

"I can borrow one, yeah."

"Okay, let's go."

"What about Mike?" Reg asked.

"I looked for him, I couldn't find him anywhere."

"All right. Let's move."

They caught the next bus up the hill, walked two blocks to a big house. "I rent a room here," Reg said. "I'll just run in and see if I can borrow the car."

They went up the steps and in through a door with beautiful stained-glass flowers inlaid in the glass. The hall was all polished wood, with several mailboxes on the wall. They went up the wooden stairs, which ended in a long hallway. Reg knocked on the first door and a man opened it. "Sebastien, I'm glad you're home. May I borrow your car? A friend of mine has an emergency. Regan, this is Sebastien, a fellow student from the university."

"Guess so," said Sebastien, yawning. "Got to finish that last essay rewrite and then go on to better things. Come on inside while I find the keys."

Regan stepped into the room behind Reg and looked around. She took a deep breath. One whole wall of the room was lined with books. A wooden desk was near the windows, which had blue velvet drapes. There was a big comfortable-looking office chair and a woven rug in deep red, blue and purple. Through an adjoining door she could see a big bed with a deep blue duvet and blue satin sheets, and through another door, what appeared to be a small kitchen. The walls that didn't have books on them had paintings, big splashy flowers in bright colours. There was even a small fireplace and a fireplace mantel with a giant bouquet of flowers.

Regan knew instantly that this was the kind of room she could live in. This was a room straight out of one of the English novels she had read at school. She stared at the books while Sebastien rummaged through various pockets and under cushions and in glass jars.

"Sorry, sorry, I never drive the thing enough to remember where I threw the keys. I really should have a place for them, I suppose."

Finally, the keys turned up in a wooden box on the desk. Sebastien handed them to Reg. "Here, have fun, don't run into anything. The old man would have a fit."

The "thing" turned out to be a small, black, racy-looking car. They got in and Reg figured out how to start it. He ground the gears and the car jerked once or twice until he got it under control. "I don't drive much here," he said. "I used to have a car in Ireland but it was ancient. I think it was the same age as my grandfather. So, do you know where we are going?"

"Yes," said Regan. "I'll give you directions as we go."

"We're just going to drive by," Reg said. "We're not stopping. And you keep your head down. If the police see you there, we're both in trouble."

"Right," said Regan.

They rode in silence. "So who is Sebastien?" Regan asked.

"Oh, he just rents a room in that house, same as me. We've become friends. Sometimes we study together. He's almost finished school, already got a good job in some big university in America. His daddy owns lots of things, a furniture store, and a brewery, or something. I can never keep it straight."

"I like his room."

"Yeah, me too. He has lots of money, and at least he's never cheap, always good for a loan or a beer or borrowing the car."

Regan stared out the window. It was completely dark now. She wished she knew where Mike had gone. She got out her laptop and gave directions to Reg. While she had it open, she read the email from the editor.

"Great piece," it read. "Will be running it next week. We can pay $350. Please send invoice."

She read the email to Reg. "What's an invoice?" she asked.

"Your bill," he said. He was distracted, peering through the windshield into the dark, trying to decipher street signs.

"$350," she said. "Wow! Do they pay all writers that much?"

"Depends."

"On what?"

"On the publication, on the number of words, on how much they like it. Some don't pay at all, some pay a lot."

"You mean you can make a living writing stuff?"

"Well, some people do. That's mostly what I do, write stuff and hand it in to the university. And if I do it right, I get a degree and eventually, a job. What was that address again?"

She read it to him. "Turn right, up there."

They could see lights now. It was raining hard again and almost dark. Coloured flashing lights bounced and jittered off the windshield.

"Oh no, what's going on?" Regan cried. There were police cars, fire trucks, yellow emergency vehicles, and ambulances. "Stop, Reg, stop. Let me out!"

"No way," he said. "You promised. Keep your head down."

"But the house! It's on fire."

"Is it? No, it's just the lights reflecting."

"Then why are there fire engines? No, look, there's smoke. I smell smoke."

"Oh, the fire engines just come with the cops. I think."

"Look, there's cops everywhere. What's that white van?"

"It says something," Reg said. He peered through the window. "Hazardous materials . . . why would they be here? Is there a bomb or something?"

"A bomb!"

"No, no, don't be scared, Regan. They are probably just here as backup. I think they just come out as part of the team. You know, they try to think of everything." Reg tried to make his voice soothing and calm but Regan could hear the fear in it.

Reg drove the car at a slow crawl along the edge of the road, trying to get past the cluster of emergency vehicles. A tall cop waved him past and they made it to the next intersection and stopped. Another cop was standing there directing traffic. As soon as they stopped, Regan hit the unlock button, shoved open the door, jumped out of the car, and rolled down the bank and into a swampy ditch. Thorns and brush caught at her clothes, scratched her face and hands.

"Regan, no." She could hear Reg calling. Cars began to honk. She crawled on her hands and knees along the edge of the slimy water in the bottom of the ditch. She could hear footsteps running along the pavement above her, but the bottom of the ditch was shadowed by overhanging brush on the edge of the road. The ditch itself was full of reeds and tall grass and she couldn't see much of anything, except for little bits of flashing, reflected light on the thin line of water in the bottom of the ditch. Flashlight beams crossed and recrossed the ditch. She squatted under a clump of thick willows, pulled the thin dangling branches in around her, and hid her face in her knees. Someone even squelched by her in the ditch, his boots squeaking and sucking at the mud, but even when he flashed his light at the sides of the ditch, he didn't see her. It helped that she was wearing black.

Eventually the noise and voices receded and she became brave enough to crawl out of her hiding place. She stood up to shake the cramps out of her legs, then knelt down and began to crawl on her hands and knees. When she thought she had gone far enough to be opposite the house, she clambered carefully up the bank, digging in her fingers to hold on, and peered over the edge of the bank.

She was directly opposite a cluster of cops standing in the middle of the road. They were close together, talking and gesturing towards the house. From their voices it sounded as if they were arguing, but she couldn't hear what they were saying. She did catch the words, "chemical," "blow," and "wait."

She could see now that the house really was on fire. It was a huge house, set back from the road on about an acre of land, and surrounded by a high chain-link fence. There were two enormous dogs inside the fence, barking and jumping at the wire. The gate was closed and she could see a broken padlock and chain hanging from it.

She ducked back down into the ditch and headed for the far end of the street. She couldn't see very well, and twice she fell in the water and had to climb out, clawing at the mud and grass to get back up on the bank. Finally, when she judged that she was far enough away, she crawled up the bank again. She had to dig her fingers in like claws to lever herself up and onto the road. She flopped belly-down onto the gravel and watched to see if any of the cops reacted. No one seemed to be looking in her direction. She leapt to her feet, raced across the road, and flung herself into the ditch on the other side. She rolled down the bank into the water. She was thoroughly soaked now, and covered with water and mud. She pushed strands of wet muddy hair out of her eyes.

She splashed as quietly as she could through the ditch, crawled up the other side, and emerged on top, just in front of a huge cedar hedge that fronted the yard next to the burning house. Quickly, she ran along the hedge to where it met the chain link fence surrounding the neighbouring yard. Yes, there was a space there, between the hedge and the fence, just narrow enough to squeeze through.

She made it into the yard and followed the fence towards the back of the house. The dogs were still distracted, leaping and barking like crazy things against the front fence gate. There were several large trees growing on the neighbour's side of the fence, enormous trees with limbs that stuck out over the fence. But the branches were too high to reach. She slowed down and looked more closely. Finally, she found one tree with branches low enough that if she leapt up, she could just get her hands on them. She jumped, grabbed, swung her legs up, perched on the branch, peered through the bare branches and twigs at the cops. Still, no one appeared to have noticed anything. She couldn't see flames in the house but smoke appeared to be billowing out of one of the upstairs windows. No one was doing anything. Why were the cops just standing around in the middle of the road?

Now there appeared to be some movement. Yet another enormous white van had appeared, and a crew of people were getting out of it and dressing themselves in white suits, white hats, white boots. Suddenly there was an explosion in the upstairs of the house and now flames did appear, shooting out of a broken window.

Oh no, she thought. Time to move, and fast. She crawled out on the branch, over the fence, swung down, dropped to her feet and ran as fast as she could for the back of the house.

She heard a shout. She must have been spotted by someone. As she ran to the house, several security motion lights went on.

The dogs heard her as well. The tone of their barking changed. She risked a quick glance. Yes, they were coming for her. She had almost made it to the back door which was actually a set of sliding doors that, it now appeared, someone had left wide open. She leapt through the doors and slammed them shut in the face of the snarling dogs, just in time. But now she had another problem. It was pitch black inside the house and the air was full of weirdly stinking smoke. She began to choke and cough. What had they said in all those stupid fire drills in school? Right. The floor. She fell on the floor, rolled to the glass doors and cracked them open enough so a stream of fresh air came in. She took a deep breath. The dogs sniffed and snuffled at the crack in the door, but didn't try to come in. They lost interest and took off again, probably to bark at the fire trucks and police some more. Coughing, she opened the door even wider and took several deep breaths. Now what? And where was everyone? Why was the house so dark and empty?

Another explosion. A ball of heat and smoke came rolling into the room from what had to be the stairs. Should she go up there? But there was already too much smoke and flame. If anyone were still alive, they would be in the basement. So if those were the stairs going up, where were the stairs going down? There, in that black space. That had to be where the stairs were.

She slid off her soaking wet muddy t-shirt and wrapped

it around her face, leaving only her eyes free. And then she got to her feet and staggered for the stairs. As she felt her way down the stairs, the air got fresher. Of course, the smoke was staying upstairs. She came to the bottom, felt along the wall. Yes, a light switch. She flipped it on and was rewarded by a glow from a single overhead bulb. There was still so much smoke that the light shone a dim orange. She was in a basement of some kind. A corridor stretched ahead of her with several doors. She tried each of the doors, all locked. The last door at the end was also locked, but as she tried the knob, she heard voices, women's voices.

"Help!" someone called and was joined by a chorus of voices. "Help us," they called. "Help, help!"

Desperately, she rattled the knob and pushed on the door. She stepped back, took a deep breath and then another one. The smoke got in her lungs and made her cough. The smoke was getting thicker. She could hear Sifu's voice in her head. "Centre, concentrate, breathe."

She bent over, took several deep breaths using the t-shirt to mask her mouth. Then she backed up and ran at the door, hit it with both feet and fell back to the floor. The door hadn't opened but the edge, where the lock was, had bent. She backed up, bent over, took several more breaths, squared herself, yelled at the top of her lungs as she ran, hit the door again with both feet square, and then tumbled inside as the door burst open.

Screams. Voices. Moaning. This room, too, was full of smoke

but a bit less than the corridor. A group of women, Asian women mostly, young women, from the looks of things. Not her mother.

"Come on," she said. "We've got to get out of here. The house is on fire." They stared at her. They didn't understand the words but they heard the urgency in her voice. They crowded towards the door.

"Wait," called a voice. There was a babble of words in some language Regan couldn't understand, and then one of the women gestured to a back room. They pointed at Regan, pointed at another door towards the back of the room. Regan shouldered her way through them as they shoved their way past her out the door.

The door to the back room wasn't locked. Regan turned the knob, peered in. It was dark in the room but there was a high barred window with light leaking in from the outside security lights. Someone was lying on a mattress on the floor, under the window.

Regan ran across the room, dropped to her knees. "Mom? Mommy?" The woman on the mattress moaned. Her eyes were closed. She whispered something Regan couldn't hear. Regan leaned over, put her head on her mom's chest. There was a rough, stained bandage tied around her mom's arm.

"Regan," her mom whispered. "My queenie, my princess. What are you doing here? Am I dead? Is this a dream?"

"No, Mom, I'm really here. I broke in. The house is on fire. We've got to get out. You've got to get up."

"I don't know if I can. My arm . . ."

Just then, Regan heard screams and the thunder of feet and the Asian women came rushing back into the room. They yelled at her and then one, who spoke some broken English said, "Fire, is fire, up there." She gestured back towards the stairs.

Regan left her mom, ran to the corridor, ran to the foot of the stairs. She could see smoke and flames at the top of the stairs. Then another explosion sent smoke and what looked like a ball of fire rolling down the stairs towards her. She slammed the door and ran to the back room. The women crowded in around her.

"Up, lift me up." She gestured at the window, made lifting motions. One woman ran to the window, bent over and put her hands on her knees, gestured for Regan to stand on her back. Another helped her step on the back of the bent woman. She could just reach the high barred window. She wrapped what was left of her t-shirt around her fist and punched the glass out. It took a few tries and then it broke. She pulled and wiggled at the bars. They were loose but not very much. She needed some leverage, something.

She leapt down, looked around the room. "Tools?" she asked. The faces stared back at her. "Hammer?"

Then the one who spoke some English said, "Ahh, hammer. Yes." She ran out of the room, returned in a moment with a broken piece of thick wood.

"Yes," Regan said. She ran back to the kneeling woman, leapt on her back, slipped the wood under the bottom of the bars, pushed it up so it would work as a lever, pulled with all her might. It wouldn't budge. "Help me," she yelled at the women, gaping at her with their mouths open. "Come and help."

Instead, they huddled together, weeping and holding on to each other. But the older one, the one who had fetched the stick, reached up, grabbed onto the wood, and added her weight to Regan's strength. Together, they slowly pried the bars away from the window.

But the window was tiny. Could she get through it? She had to try. She cleared away the broken glass with her sleeve, reached up, grabbed the window sill, got her head through, slithered and kicked and shoved and slid onto the ground outside. She scrambled to her feet and ran towards the flashing lights and the waiting fire trucks.

And the dogs. The dogs who came running, barking, snarling, but then someone opened the gate and whistled. The dogs heard the whistle, stopped, wheeled around looked up, ran for the open gate and disappeared down the road.

The policemen had seen her. One raised his gun. Another grabbed his arm to stop him.

"There's people in the house," she yelled at them. "Women. Help us! They're trapped in the basement. There's no one else there. Hurry, hurry!" She was screaming now. Her hands were bleeding where she had torn them open on the glass in the window sill. She had forgotten she was soaking wet and covered in mud. "My mom is there, my mom is there!"

Finally, finally, they were all moving, jumping on the fire trucks, driving them though the gate, men running alongside, pulling hoses and axes and oxygen masks and ladders off the trucks. The white vans moved as well, coming in the gate, along with the men in white baggy suits.

"Hurry," she screamed at the men. "Hurry."

They pulled on oxygen masks. They followed her around the side of the house. She could hear the women screaming and the men could hear them now as well.

Men began smashing at the house wall with axes. A fireman grabbed her. "Kid, you need to get out of here," he yelled at her. "It's a chemical fire. It could blow at anytime."

"My mom is in there," she yelled back. "She can't move. She's hurt. Get her out. Get her out now." She was crying. She began to pound at his yellow slickered chest. "Get her out, get her out." She couldn't breathe. She began to cough and choke. She gagged so hard she thought she was going to throw up.

He picked her up as if she weighed nothing, carried her to the fence, and dumped her over it. Somehow, Reg was there with paramedics. They grabbed her and put her on a stretcher. She fought them.

"No, Reg, my mom, my mom is in there. Go see. Go make them get her out. Don't let them take me away until I see my mom is safe."

They were trying to fit an oxygen mask over her face and she was fighting, crying, screaming, coughing so hard she thought she might never catch her breath.

"Leave me alone," she yelled, when she finally got a breath. "Get my mom, get my mom."

"It's okay," a voice said by her ear. "They've got her. They're inside. They're getting all the women out of there. How the hell did you do that?"

It was Brenda. "We've got her," she said again. "We've got your mom. She's safe."

Regan lay back on the stretcher. She was still shaking and coughing. She let them put the oxygen mask over her face. But when they went to put her in an ambulance, she pulled it off, and yelled again. "Not without my mom."

"Wait," Brenda said impatiently to the paramedics, in her authoritative police voice. "Just wait until her mom is here."

"She needs to get to the hospital," said one of the paramedics.

"She needs her mother," Brenda snapped. "She just saved a whole house full of women. Now leave her alone."

And then somehow, Brenda was holding her hand and stroking her hair. "You little idiot," she said, her voice full of wonder. "Sifu was right. You're a tough smart kid. And you're a total, freaking idiot. Please, never, ever do that again."

And, then finally, Regan's mom was on a stretcher next to her, they were both loaded in an ambulance, side by side, and from far away, Regan heard the ambulance start up, heard the siren. She reached out, and her mother took her hand. Regan smiled and closed her eyes.

Chapter Eleven

TEN DAYS LATER, Regan was at the hospital by nine in the morning. She followed the red line down the long hall to the elevator and went up to her mom's room.

Her mom was sitting up in bed. "Baby," she said. "Oh, it is so good to see you. Every time I see you, I think, who is this gorgeous girl? Oh yeah, it's my beautiful daughter." She patted the bed beside her and Regan sat down, then lay back on the pillows.

"Mommy, I have a little surprise for you," she said.

"What, what is it?"

"Not until we go home. You can't see it until then."

"C'mon, give me a hint."

"Nope."

"A teensy, weensy, little tiny hint."

"Nope."

"But I can't go home until Dr. Cameron looks in. The nurse said he was doing his rounds and would get here as soon as he could. Can I wait that long for my surprise?"

"Guess you are going to have to."

Her mom pretended to sulk and then she laughed and then she and Regan talked about other things.

"It's weird, living with Brenda," Regan said. "She turned out to be really nice. She said if I win the tournament, she'll take me shopping. Even though she's a cop, she said she would never let any friend of hers have to stay in a group home. She said that's why she told the social workers that I was staying with her. "

The social worker who had interviewed Regan at the police station had seemed to think it was entirely reasonable that she should go back to the group home. They wouldn't let her stay at Sifu's studio because no one was there at night to supervise her.

"I won't go there," Regan had told her. "I'll go sleep on a bench in the rain before I'll go there."

Brenda had intervened. "She's staying with me," she said. "We've already talked about it. I'll take full responsibility. Just until her mom comes home."

Regan and her mom also talked about school, and the massive piles of homework that were probably waiting for

Regan when she did go back. Regan kept watching her mom's face. It was thinner and her eyes seemed haunted somehow. She kept watching the door, and jumped at every unexpected sound. Her laugh was a little too loud, her voice too cheerful. Finally she dozed off and Regan stood up and sat in a chair in the corner of the room.

There was a knock on the door and a woman came in.

"Hi Regan, I'm Jennifer Johnson, the hospital social worker. We need to have a little chat before your mom goes home."

Regan didn't want to chat, but she followed the woman anyway. Jennifer was young, blond, and smiling. Her clothes looked brand new, a red velvet shirt tucked into tailored black pants. Her teeth were perfect. She wore just the right amount of makeup. High-heeled shoes. They went down a floor and into an office with grey carpeting, a desk, and two chairs.

"Now, I realize you and your mom have been through a terrible ordeal," said Jennifer briskly after she sat down. "Do you want to talk about it?"

Regan stood in front of the desk. She shook her head.

Jennifer waited for a few seconds and then went on. "Well, I am sure it was quite hard for you both. My sympathies are with you. You should know that your mother may exhibit some symptoms of post-traumatic stress when she goes home, lack of sleep, short temper, that sort of thing. It may take quite a long while for her to recover. Her doctor has given her a prescription for some medication that should help. My suggestion would be that you and your mother both get some counsel-ling, separately and together. Do you have any questions?"

Regan shook her head again.

"Okay. Here's my card. Feel free to call me if you have any further questions or need help with anything."

She stood up. Regan shuffled out the door, tore the card into ribbons, threw it in a trash can and then went back to sit by her mother's bed.

Finally, Dr. Cameron arrived with his ongoing retinue of white-coated students fluttering around him. They reminded Regan of seagulls, anxiously peering around him at her mother as if she was a tasty bit of leftover bun. He checked her mom's pulse, listened to her chest, and then said, "So, what are you still doing here? Out, out of my hospital. Go home, get your life back."

"Yes," Regan exclaimed, bouncing off the end of the bed.

"I want a shower, a haircut, a decent meal, and a walk in the park, in any order," her mom said.

"Home first," Regan announced. She helped her mom out of the bed and held her clothes for her to get dressed. She had brought some clean clothes and underwear with her because her mom's clothes smelled of smoke and chemicals, and the hospital had thrown them out.

The nurse called a taxi for them. They held hands down the hall and into the elevator. Regan's mom walked very slowly. Outside, she kept her eyes down on the sidewalk while they waited for the taxi.

Regan paid for the cab fare herself with the money from her newspaper column. When they got to the apartment building, she helped her mom out of the taxi, then opened the apartment front door and led the way up the stairs. Her mom had to lean on the stairs halfway up and catch her breath. Then Regan opened the front door.

"Surprise!"

Her mom stopped in the doorway. "Regan," she said. "It's the wrong place. Someone else must have moved in. Oh, no, what are we going to do now?" Her face twisted as if she were going to cry.

"No, mom, it's our place. Reg's friends did it. Have a look."

"Really? Are you sure?"

"Reg has this friend Sebastien. His dad owns a furniture store. He and a bunch of other graduate students gave us new furniture. They said it was kind of a reward."

Her mom wandered from room to room in wonder, trailing her hand over the velvet sofa, the soft blue drapes, the shining glass coffee table, the new kitchen set. She went in both bedrooms, looked at the new beds, complete with duvets.

Finally, she stopped. "Regan honey, is there any food in this place?"

Proudly, Regan opened the fridge door. "They thought of everything."

"Then can you please make me a really good cup of coffee, with cream and honey. I can't remember the last time I had a decent cup of coffee."

Regan filled the new percolator, and when the coffee was done, she served it to her mother and herself in brand new mugs, with cream and honey, and oatmeal cookies on a plate. They sat together, staring out the window at the familiar sight.

Finally her mom said, "Let's go out for a celebratory lunch." They dressed up, started down the stairs and as soon as they got to the street, Regan's mom leaned against the wall of the building, her face white, and her hands shaking. It was all Regan could do to get her back in the apartment. She took her mom's hand and led her back inside, step by step, like a young child.

"Regan," her mom said after she sat down again at the kitchen table. "I've been thinking about when I can go back to work, but if I can't even go outside, I'm sure never going to survive a day full of strange people."

"Mom, you just need to rest for a while. I can take care of you. I could even get a job."

"No, Regan, you are going back to school. We can get by on my disability payments for a while. But I need something else to think about. Otherwise the horror of that burning house and what could have happened will keep going around in my head."

Regan hesitated. She had so many questions that were still unanswered.

Her mom looked at her. "Regan, you need to hear the whole story. But right now, it's just so hard to talk about."

"I know, Mom. It's just, I don't get why they took you in the first place. I don't know where you were or what happened. I keep thinking about it. I can't make the questions stop."

Her mom sighed. She put her chin in her hands and stared out the window. "Clayton said it would be fun, just a card game, I'd get some money for serving drinks and be home again. But I figured out pretty quick that the guys at the card game were gangsters. I overheard them talking. I tried not to listen, just kept my head down. But then the money disappeared and it was chaos. I heard George yelling and I got away and I hid. I had a little bit of money but not enough. I was afraid to contact anyone so I hid in some pretty crazy places." Her eyes went wide. "I slept under bridges. I even rode the train. I can't stand to think about it."

She was silent. Then she started up again. "They found me one day when I was going through a garbage bin, looking for food. They thought either I'd taken the money or I knew who did. So they beat me up and locked me in the basement of that house and tried to make me talk. I told them over and over I didn't know anything. Finally, they threw me in that back room and left me there. They didn't care if I lived or died. Their stupid drug lab meant the air in the whole house was full of toxic chemicals. I got sicker and sicker. Then one night, one of the woman snuck in and told me she was leaving. One of the dealers was taking her with him. I didn't have any way to send you a message. They took everything away from me, but somehow, like some tiny miracle, I had that silly sheet of stickers in the pocket of my jacket. It slipped into the lining and they had overlooked it. So I sent it with her, not knowing if you would ever see it."

Regan's mom started to cry. "I'm so sorry, Regan, for what I put you through. Oh, what you must have gone through, all alone."

"It's okay, Mom. It's okay. People helped. People looked after me."

She wondered if she would ever tell her mom what she had really been through. So far, her mom hadn't asked.

No one had been arrested after the fire. Regan had asked Brenda about it, but Brenda said everyone involved had simply disappeared. Someone at the house had spotted that they were being watched by the police and had taken a shot at a police car. The police had started to go into the house but more gunshots were fired. The gang members escaped out the back and even though police cars took off after them, the gang cars simply outran the cops. Then the fire broke out. The police had no idea there were women trapped in the house. The police assumed that it was a chemical fire from a drug lab. They were afraid it would blow up. That was why they hadn't entered the house.

"I don't know how to put this, Regan," Brenda had told her. "They were selling those women. Plus manufacturing and selling drugs."

"They left my mom in that room to die," Regan said. "When she tried to escape, they beat her up and broke her arm. How can people be that cruel?"

Brenda shook her head. "I don't understand it either," she said. "But that's why I'm a cop. I do what I can to stop people like that. It's never enough, but it's what I can do."

Most of the women who had been in the house were now in the process of going through refugee claims. Some had gone home. Some had disappeared into the streets.

"Regan, I have got to lie down," her mom said. Her eyes were wide. "Please make sure the doors are locked. Please."

"Sure, Mom."

She wandered off to the bedroom and Regan watched her go. Her mom still limped and she seemed dizzy. She held on to the door of her room for a moment before she made it to the bed. When Regan checked on her later, she was curled up with the duvet pulled up over the side of her head and just her face showing. There was a bottle of sleeping pills on the bureau beside the bed.

Regan thought about what the counsellor had said. All along she had thought only about getting her mother back. She had assumed that everything would go back to normal: they would get their lives back, Regan would go back to school, and her mom would go back to work. It wasn't going to be that simple.

She got her laptop, cruised through messages, updates, websites, and then took a look at her own latest column on the newspaper website with the name, "Runner," beneath it.

There was a short biography of her on the website but it only said she was fourteen and lived downtown. Only a few people who read the column would ever have any idea who she really was. Reg had told her that being a writer was like being invisible and naked at the some time. It made her self-conscious and yet free to say whatever she wanted. Maybe she should try to write something more demanding than just a newspaper column. Maybe a story or even a book? But how did anyone go about writing a book? Maybe they just wrote it and then figured it out. She started typing.

When her mom got up, they made dinner together; there was frozen lasagna in the freezer and a loaf of French bread. Regan's mom seemed better. They ate dinner, watched television, and went to bed. Regan fell asleep quickly.

She woke screaming from a nightmare of burning and smoke. She sat up in the bed and her mother came running from the other room. She grabbed Regan and held on tight.

They didn't say a word, just held each other.

"Nightmare," Regan whispered finally. "It's okay, Mom, I'm fine."

"Well, I'm not," her mother said. "Come and curl up with me. We can tell each other stories to get back to sleep."

Regan crawled into her mother's big bed. They lay side by side.

"This isn't going to be easy, honey," her mother said at last. "They told me at the hospital it would take a while to recover. It's called PTSD, post-traumatic stress disorder. Soldiers get it, apparently. Guess they weren't kidding. I've been lying awake most of the night, watching the door, too scared to sleep."

"That social worker was an idiot."

"Yeah, but an educated idiot. They're the very best kind."

"Hey, Mom, let's have some hot chocolate and watch old movies."

"Sounds like a plan, Stan."

"With whipped cream."

"Ooh, yeah."

They fell asleep at four in the morning, with the television blaring and all the lights in the apartment still on.

Chapter Twelve

REGAN STOOD IN THE door of the girls' dressing room in the high school gymnasium, watching the bleachers fill up with people. She watched for Mike, hoping against hope that he would make it. She hadn't seen him since the fire and her mom's rescue. She had looked for him in all the usual places but he wasn't there and no one had seen him. Reg told her not to worry, that Mike would turn up sooner or later. Brenda just said, "He'll be fine. Mike's a survivor."

And she was watching for her mother.

Reg had assured Regan he would pick up her mom, drive her to the auditorium, stay right beside her and drive her home again as soon as the tournament was over. Now, Regan saw them come into the auditorium. Her mom was hanging on tightly to Reg's arm, but she seemed to be walking easily. She and Reg were even talking and laughing.

Regan went back into the change room, found a corner that wasn't quite as chaotic as the rest of the room, sat down, and closed her eyes. Deliberately and carefully, she went through all the steps of her pattern in her mind, visualizing each move, each kick and punch, each turn. When she was done, she breathed calmly, quietly, thinking through each of Sifu's instructions. She was ready.

She went outside to the auditorium, and waited with the rest of the kids from her group. Several smiled at her but no one made conversation. Everyone was too tense. Regan watched the other fighters carefully. Every so often, she stood up and went through a few stretches and kicks to keep her muscles warm.

And now it was her turn. She walked to the ring, bowed to the judges and to Sifu, then backed up and centred herself. She took three deep breaths and then launched into her routine. It went by in a blur: kick, block, punch, turn, centre, do it again and again. There was no time to think. And then, in what seemed a blink of an eye, she was done. She bowed again, turned and walked back to her chair and sat down, puffing hard.

She had one more event, an actual demonstration fight. She and the other fighter wouldn't touch each other but they would do everything but. As she heard her name being called, she stood up and there was Mike, walking into the hall with some older woman. He hadn't seen her yet. She wanted to run over to him, hug him, tell him how much she had missed him.

Instead, she squared her shoulders, breathed, centred her body, walked slowly and carefully, eyes down, to the centre of the gym, bowed to the judges, and then bowed to her opponent. But she was flustered and couldn't concentrate properly and she knew it. She fought furiously, but her moves were either too slow or too fast, her turns were ragged. Her opponent, slightly taller and stronger than her, could sense her lack of timing. Gradually, Regan was forced to retreat, forced more and more off balance. She stepped back, took a second, breathing hard, then forced herself to concentrate.

Flames licked around her face and arms, smoke rasped in her lungs. She would not quit, she would not fail. She would never quit, even after she was turned into ashes. She stormed back, kicking, punching, high, fast, straight, one punch after another, clear, clean, until the referee separated them and she stepped back, bowed, furious and red-faced, and left the ring.

Now she could look at Mike, and he could look at her. She waved, smiled, sat down in her chair, managed to sit still until it was break time, and then, finally, she could make it through the crowd to Mike.

She held onto him for a long time.

"This is my Aunt Ruby," he said when she let go. "My mom's sister. I'm going back with her, tomorrow, back home. Took me a while to find her, and then I found out she was looking for me. So it worked out."

"That's great," she said, and meant it. She studied him. His hair was cut, and his lean face looked more tanned than usual. He was wearing new clothes.

"Nice clothes."

"Yeah, Auntie got them."

Aunt Ruby smiled and said nothing.

"Listen, stay in touch. I'll miss you. You know that. I owe you so much. I can never thank you enough."

"I owe you too," he said quietly. "Yeah, I'll miss you."

"Friends," she said.

"You know it. You taught me about friendship. And staying true to yourself."

"I gotta go check on my mom," Regan said. "She has a hard time with crowds. It's going to take her a while to deal with everything."

"Yeah, I know. I'm glad I saw you fight. You were amazing."

"Thanks." She put her arms around him again, held on. He put his arms around her, held on hard. She pulled back, looked at him. Their eyes met. Regan felt warmth flood through her. He was staring at her so hard. I'm not ready for this, she thought. Not yet.

She let go, her face red, and turned to hug Aunt Ruby, who squashed her in what felt like the warmest, squishiest hug ever, and then she forced herself to walk away, walk back to where her mom was waiting for her on the bleachers. She sat down beside her mom, who grabbed her hand and held on tight.

"I'm going to go home now," she whispered. "I am so glad

I was here. So glad. So proud, Regan." She started to cry, then stood up and stumbled down the bleacher stairs. Regan stood up but Reg just said, "I got it. I'll take her home. You stay. You need to wait for the results."

Regan watched him run after her mom and take her arm. Her mom turned and leaned her head on Reg's shoulder, hiding her face. Then she straightened herself and the two of them left the auditorium together. Regan sat down on the bleachers, cupped her chin in her hands, tried to appear to take an interest in what the other competitors were doing. When they announced that she had won her division, she stood up, came down the bleachers, bowed to the judges, and accepted her ribbon. Then she walked with measured steps to the dressing room to change. As soon as she got her street clothes on, she headed for home.

Her mother was asleep when she got there, and there was no sign of Reg. Regan sat in the dark apartment, staring out the window. Carefully, she placed the ribbon from the tournament on the table where her mom would find it in the morning. Tomorrow she would get up early, dress in her new clothes, go to school, and come home again. A normal life, Regan thought, or as normal as it was ever going to be.

Chapter Thirteen

SATURDAY MORNING IN the spring, and it wasn't raining. In fact, the sun was out, shining on the city, and the streets were almost dry. Regan bounced out of bed. Her mom was still sleeping.

Regan had practice with Sifu this morning so she made herself a good breakfast: yogurt and toast and fruit. It was still early when she finished eating. She threw on a jacket, and ran out the door and down the apartment stairs.

Her mom would probably sleep late. The sleeping pills made her groggy in the morning. Last night, she and her mom had stayed up late watching a movie. When the movie was over, Regan's mom said, "I called your grandma. She wants to come for a visit. I said that would be good."

"Wow, Mom, that would be wonderful."

"And I've also been talking to my counsellor about my future, and yours. I'm feeling so much better. Plus I talked to Reg about going to school. He's been so helpful. There are some courses I'd like to take. I've been looking at them. Remember when I was going to be an accountant? Well, apparently, I can take all those courses online. I'm going to try, Regan. I really am. It will be hard and it is still going to take a while to get over this but I think I can do it. I hope I can."

"That's so cool, Mom." Regan threw her arms around her mother and hugged her hard.

Regan sauntered along the sidewalk, her face upturned to the sun. Far above, birds were wheeling and screaming in the blue sky. She looked more closely. It was an eagle, being harassed by a cloud of gulls and crows. She looked around. Most people were hurrying by with their faces down. No one else saw the eagle. The eagle spiralled higher in the sky and the flocks of gulls and crows fell away.

She decided to go by the park where Mike used to juggle. It was on her way to the dojo; she could grab a coffee from the café there, maybe sit in the sun for a few minutes. When she came around the corner, she stopped, half-hoping to see him. No, he wasn't there. That was good, she thought. He was with his family where he should be.

She went to the small stand near the park, got a coffee from the coffee shop, sat in the sun on the concrete wall around the park, and watched the people go by.

"Hey lady, got any change?" She looked up. It was Zack. He was smiling and seemed sober. He sat down beside her and pulled his shopping cart close to him.

"So I heard on the street what happened," he said. "You're starting to turn into a bit of a legend down here."

"Wow, Zack, it's so good to see you. How's Ramona and everybody?"

"Ramona? She's doin' okay. She's got a new doctor, got her on some new pills. Seem to be helping."

"Please say hi for me. Are you going back to the camp in the spring?"

"Maybe, not sure yet. I'll let you know."

"It was peaceful there."

"Yeah, it was. You take care of yourself. I'll be keepin' my ears open for news about you. And I'll say hi to folks for you."

"Thanks, Zack. Sorry, I have to go to class right now."

"And me, I got bottles to pick." He stood up, started to push his jangling cart away and then turned back.

"Say, Regan, just remembered. I heard from that Mike kid you used to hang with. He's back on the streets, but apparently he's goin' to that university school they got down here."

"He's back?"

"Yeah." Zack hesitated. "The streets, they get in your blood, Regan. He said his family was always preaching at him and he had to leave. But he's doin' good. He's clean, even has a job and a place to stay. He said he'd sure like to see you but he's scared. Thinks you might be mad at him for coming back." Zack laughed. "He has class every Thursday night at the community centre. I thought you might want to know." Zack started to walk away and then turned back. "I think he's got a thing for you. Maybe you for him too, eh?" He laughed again.

Regan stood up to go. "Zack, please tell him hi for me. Tell him I am still his friend. Now, and always. Thanks, Zack."

She walked on towards the dojo, smiling to herself. She heard the shrill whistling again. High in the sky, alone, the eagle circled and circled on its broad wings, mounting higher and higher into the sky, until it was only a speck, and then it disappeared.

SIFU'S KUNG FU RULES

GON: Everyday, without neglect, do your training.

DAN: Be brave and calm in order to make the right decisions.

JIE: Judge yourself without conceit and do not act thoughtlessly.

YI: Act without hesitation and do what is right.

ABOUT THE AUTHOR

Luanne Armstrong lives on her farm on Kootenay Lake in British Columbia. She is the author of many books for both adults and younger readers, and she currently teaches Creative Writing online for the University of British Columbia. Her young adult novel *Jeannie and the Gentle Giants*, published by Ronsdale in 2001, was nominated for the prestigious Silver Birch Award. Her second novel with Ronsdale, *Pete's Gold*, was a Moonbeam finalist and was shortlisted for the Chocolate Lily and Red Cedar Awards. It was also selected as a Best Book by the Canadian Children's Book Centre. For a number of years she was co-publisher of Hodgepog Books. *I'll Be Home Soon* was inspired by her many experiences teaching and working with young people and listening to their stories.

Website: www.luannearmstrong.ca
Email: luannearmstrong@wynndel.ca

RECYCLED
Paper made from
recycled material
FSC® C103567

Marquis Book Printing Inc.

Québec, Canada
2012

Printed on Silva Enviro 100% post-consumer EcoLogo certified paper,
processed chlorine free and manufactured using biogas energy.